IMMERSION

IMMERSION: AN ASIAN ANTHOLOGY OF LOVE, FANTASY, AND SPECULATIVE FICTION

RICEPAPER MAGAZINE BOOKS VOLUME 2

JF GARRARD   ALLAN CHO   WILLIAM THAM

DARK HELIX
PRESS

Asian Canadian Writers Workshop publishes Ricepaper Magazine year round online. Visit Ricepapermagazine.ca for more details.

For permission requests, in correspondence, please send to "Attention: Editor-in-Chief," at the address below.

Ricepaper Magazine PO Box 74174 Centre Point Mall PO Vancouver, BC V5T 4E7

Alternatively: info@ricepapermagazine.ca www.ricepapermagazine.ca

First Edition

Library and Archives Canada Cataloguing in Publication

Title: Immersion : an Asian anthology of love, fantasy, and speculative fiction / [edited by] JF Garrard, Allan Cho, William Tham.

Other titles: Immersion (2019) | Asian anthology of love, fantasy, and speculative fiction

Names: Garrard, J. F., 1978- editor. | Cho, Allan, editor. | Tham, William, 1991- editor.

Description: First edition. | Series statement: Ricepaper magazine books ; volume 2 | Short stories.

Identifiers: Canadiana (print) 20190171669 | Canadiana (ebook) 20190172061 | ISBN 9781988416298

(softcover) | ISBN 9781988416304 (PDF)

Subjects: LCSH: Canadian fiction—21st century. | LCSH: Asians—Fiction. | CSH: Canadian fiction

(English)—21st century. | CSH: Canadian literature (English)—Asian-Canadian authors.

Classification: LCC PS8323.A85 I46 2019 | DDC C813.6008/094—dc23

For Jim Wong-Chu

Ricepaper Magazine Books

Currents: A Ricepaper Anthology

The Seven Muses of Harry Salcedo by Vincent Ternida

Ricepaper Magazine (online)

ricepapermagazine.ca

CONTENTS

EDITORS' INTRODUCTION

Looking back, *Immersion* was an unusual project, a real step into unknown territory. Jim Wong-Chu, founder of *Ricepaper* Magazine and LiterASIAN, took the first foray into Asian speculative fiction by shining the light on this during 2015's LiterASIAN and supporting a *Ricepaper* speculative fiction issue. After his departure, we struggled trying to find a new direction on how to support writers within a new virtual literary landscape. The shift from a print world to a digital world was abrupt. Over its lifetime, the Asian Canadian Writers' Workshop (ACWW) and *Ricepaper* went from working out of a physical office in Vancouver, full of stets, editorial marks and other relics of an analog age to working on the cloud, recruiting staff from different parts of Canada and opening ourselves to international submissions.

After the call for *Immersion* submissions opened, over the course of several months, we received many excellent submissions from Canada and beyond, drawing on the spectrum of Asian experiences worldwide. The sheer diversity was quite stunning and it proved difficult to whittle down the selected stories. In the end we came down to our shortlist, and after several rounds of editing we are happy to present them here.

A constant theme throughout the stories is about how one must change to survive. Although change is difficult, adaptation can feel as natural as walking on the pavement or hailing a cab, but sometimes, one is left to grapple with the same social issues that have endured over the years. It is strange despite how everything is constantly changing around us, it is sometimes impossible to escape the past. If we extrapolated our present struggles into the future, or an alternate dimension or even a fantasy past, we would be able to draw parallels.

Perhaps that is why speculative fiction is so powerful. The settings may be different, strands of logic taken to their extremes, but at their heart they revolve around the very human issues that affect us. In imaginary worlds, we can shed light on our confusing reality. In a world dominated by fear and uncertainty, words provide a chance for us to escape. It also provides us with the opportunity to look at our own present, and to allow us to work towards a brighter future even though it may sometimes look like there is no way out.

The publication of a book, and the attendant hours of editing, designing and proofreading that it entails, requires an army of people. First off, we would like to thank the authors for their contributions. We are especially grateful for an anonymous donor who kindly donated a grant to create this book as a recognition of Jim's legacy. Although he left us for a new journey, he still remains the beacon of light which shines on, giving us hope for the future yet to come.

An unknown author once wrote, "The past cannot be changed. The future is yet in your power." We hope that with the stories presented in this book will inspire new generations to read, write and tell stories of their own making.

Sincerely, your editors,

JF, Allan, William

JANITORS

CARLO JAVIER

I t's been some time since I last played basketball and even longer since I last went to the gym, so I knew that moving the body of a full-grown man was going to be a challenge.

The man laid in a pool of his own blood in the living room of a luxurious penthouse apartment just blocks away from Vancouver, Canada's Coal Harbour. He wore a tailored navy pinstripe suit with cufflinks that probably cost as much as a week's salary from my day job. His gold watch glimmered noticeably in the dimly lit room, like a lonely star in the vast night sky. It was an Audemars, which is as much a status symbol as it is a timepiece. The place had tall ceilings, large windows, and a panoramic view of the water. Everything looked expensive and even his fridge had a screen on it. I was sure the apartment would fetch a nice price tag on the market, despite having someone murdered right by its gas fireplace. What I wasn't sure about was the body. Someone from the Underground usually gave us at least a 48-hour notice for clean-ups like these, but they never tell us who these people are and why they're killed. I've always wanted to know these things. Some context would be nice.

The dead man had several stab wounds including one right in the centre of his throat. Lorna, my boss, said that she didn't see any signs of a struggle and that the assassin was probably quite good at their job. Everything had already been disconnected, including any form of internet connection, cameras, and any other security measure that could compromise the assassin or us. She also said that the assassin might've had a sadistic side, stabbing the man a couple of times before landing the killing blow to his throat.

"They didn't need to be so messy," Joy said as she finished stitching up the first of several deep incisions on the man's gut.

"Yeah, well, work is work," Lorna said.

Joy kept closing the wounds while we cleaned the crime scene. I used to think that stitching up the cuts and stabs was pretty pointless but soon learned that leaving them unattended could lead to a worse mess for us. These days, I tend to just keep my mouth shut and focus on the work. Cleaning can be a bit of a pain, you see, and it's not like you're cleaning a messy bathroom either. Getting rid of all the blood is tough to do and tougher to stomach, but sometimes the assassin struggles and ends up in a fight. That usually results in more of a mess. For the most part, we threw away broken things and return misplaced items to their most logical places. Once, we tried to bring new picture frames to replace shattered ones, but we quickly realized we weren't getting paid enough to go through the trouble.

Although cleaners are welcomed to take the target's belongings, and some have gotten rich by being smart scavengers - Lorna doesn't let us. She likes to say that we're not thieves and that taking from the dead will bring bad omens.

"This is gonna take a little bit longer, you guys mind getting us some coffee? There's a twenty in my jacket," Joy said.

"Oh, I got it *Ate*. I have some coffee cards anyway," Steve said.

Steve and I took the maintenance elevator down to the main lobby. The elevator was smaller than we expected and I was worried that our makeshift gurney might not even fit. Taking the body down the stairs would be tough, even though Steve was a strong 5'9, 200-something pounder who worked at Gordon Food Service for two years. I figured it would also be bad for my back.

Steve's car was parked beside our getaway van by the maintenance exit. We waved to Alvin, the apartment's night manager on our way out. He used to do cleaning as well, but since he got hired at this apartment, his schedule allowed him to continue his education. I think he taught English in the Philippines. He still takes 10% whenever jobs happen in his building. Fucking guy.

Steve's red Scion FRS was kept impressively clean and still had that faint smell of a brand-new car. His phone automatically connected to the car's Bluetooth system and he played an old Filipino rock song. It was music I recognized from my childhood, even though much of it has become a blur. Sometimes I feel as if my life started when I was twelve.

"Joy's pretty good with stitching. Does she do clothes? I have something I need hemmed."

"Maybe, I dunno. I think she used to be a nurse though. I remember someone saying that," Steve said without taking his eyes off the road.

"How did Lorna know about what the killer did?"

"Oh, *Ate Lorna* used to be a detective in the Philippines, but she moved here with her son many years ago. He goes to drop-in sometimes."

"Is he any good?" I asked instinctively.

"He will be. He's only fifteen, I think he's gonna be pretty tall."

"If Lorna was a detective, couldn't she be an assassin here? She seems pretty skilled."

"Shit, that's what I keep telling her. You should tell her, she might listen to you. Fuck, you could apply to be an assassin! You studied here!"

"Henry's an assassin and I used to see him at Langara. I don't even know if he's graduated."

3

"Oh, that dude? He's like half-Norwegian, half-Dutch, half-Finnish, half-British, and barely Filipino. Dude doesn't even speak the language."

"I'm not a killer, though," I admitted.

"Well, neither is Henry. I heard he's not very good."

Other than my family and my girlfriend, Steve is basically my biggest fan. He was at commencement when I finished my English degree at Simon Fraser University and when I completed my publishing diploma at Langara College.

I had a number of Underground job offers when I graduated from SFU. A cousin at the Shangri-La said she could get me in the hotel as an information broker, but I wasn't really stoked on the idea of collecting personal information and selling them to the highest bidders of the Underground. An old friend from high school aggressively tried to recruit me to spy for the Jehovah's Witnesses, but I'm not the most personable guy and knocking on people's houses and smiling for the entirety of a five-minute conversation about God made me uncomfortable. I did always know that the Underground would field some possible opportunities for me, since I ticked off some of the boxes they liked: I was born in the Philippines, grew up and studied in Canada, and was fluent in English and Tagalog.

But my education also got me thinking about the other side. I kind of wanted to work in an office, maybe in the government where I could secure great benefits and a sustainable pension plan.

It was Steve who finally succeeded in bringing me under. I met him about eight years ago when he first moved to Canada. We both part-timed at McDonald's and ended up playing in the same rec ball league. Steve has always been great to me, probably because I helped him with English throughout his first year. He had built his own network when he got me in the janitorial agency. He knew Filipino Underground spies at McDonald's, Church's Chicken, and Winners. He knew information brokers at hotels and smugglers who worked at the airport and in cruise ships. He told me it was easy to remain anonymous as a janitor at the mall and that at least 60% of the janitors in the Greater Vancouver are Filipino. I could blend into the background at schools, universities, hospitals, malls, and other private and publicly-owned establishments.

If Steve's estimate was right, then at least half of those Filipino janitors are also cleaners for the Underground. Those who used to be doctors and nurses in the Philippines have found some financial success and professional satisfaction as medical agents. He even argued that if all the Filipinos working in the Canadian and American service industries were to take a day or two off, the Underground would implode. I never voiced my disbelief. Crime is crime - it was gonna happen no matter what. If people somehow stopped killing each other, we would either find a way to do something else or the government would define new crimes.

Not everyone is in the business though. Religion plays a heavy role in people's philosophies and since we're essentially enabling murder after murder on a weekly basis, many Catholics tend to shy away from the Underground. Hey, more shifts for us.

Joy was done stitching by the time we got back, and Lorna had almost completely cleaned off all the blood on the floor.

"Wow, you guys are already almost done," Steve said.

"Ah well, you'll be carrying the body down so it's all fair," Lorna responded.

We placed the dead body on our makeshift gurney. Even though the gym feels like a lifetime ago, I took pride in still executing proper lifting from the ground up. Or it was probably just the years of lifting milk and cream crates at McDonald's. As expected, the body couldn't fit horizontally into the elevator, so Steve and I had to hold him upright just to get down. When we hit the maintenance lobby, Alvin was already waiting by the exit doors.

"Thanks, *kuya*," Steve said.

"Oy Esteeb! We're both thirty, you know?" Alvin replied as he held the door open for us.

We had already lined the compartment space of our getaway van with layers of extra durable packaging plastic. All we had to do now was to wrap the body a couple of times. Lorna would drive it down to the Coquitlam Transfer Station, where her friend handled the disposal. Wrapping a dead body with packaging plastic wasn't easy, and I accidentally sunk my left index and middle fingers deep into one of the dead man's stitches. Blood and other disgusting fluids dripped down from my hand. Steve laughed at me for a second, then got mad at me for not having gloves. There were no faucets nearby so I used a towel, and we kept on wrapping until the man looked like a mummy wrapped in packaging plastic.

We got back to the apartment around two o'clock to help with the last bit of the cleanup. Jobs at homes are much easier because everyone's got bathrooms and you'd expect to find some basic cleaning tools. It was different when we had a job at some empty garage a couple of months back. It was cold, dark, and the only water supply was an outdoor faucet.

I rubbed my hands intensely with the dead man's pomegranate-scented hand soap, but the blood stains were resistant. The soap was nice but Lorna wouldn't let me take anything.

Before we left, Lorna placed an inconspicuous air freshener in the dead man's home. It was *sampaguita*-scented and slowly replaced the stench of death.

"You work today Joseph?" Lorna asked me.

"No, I'm off Fridays, what about you?"

"I close."

"Oh, that's not too bad."

"Yeah, here's your cut, don't spend it all on shoes."

She handed me a cheque for $1,500. Steve got the same, while Joy got an extra $500 for all the stitching she had to do.

I hopped on the getaway van with Lorna since she was going to Coquitlam anyway. Joy lived by Joyce Station, and Steve could just drop her off on his way home to New West.

"Hey Lorna, Steve said you used to be a detective. How come you're not an assassin? You seem to have the skills for it."

"*Ay nako!* I don't even know how many times I've applied for that, but they've never promoted me. Some of the regional managers say they need me at the current branch as an excuse."

"That's wack."

"You know they'll never promote me because I didn't study here, and my work experience is just working as a nanny and as a janitor."

"You were a detective."

"Yeah, in the Philippines. Plus, even if I did get promoted, I'd get a crazy schedule and I need to cook and clean since my son isn't doing any of that."

"Steve said I should apply."

"You can. If you get in, the regional managers will train you on how to handle all sorts of guns and knives. They'll even teach you close quarter combat."

I couldn't sleep that night. I had been cleaning with Lorna, Joy, and Steve once or twice a week for the better part of the last four months, but I doubt I'll ever get used to the sight of a dead body. The smell still lingers on occasion and sometimes I catch myself looking at my fingernails in case I'd gotten any blood on them. The schedule has been bad for my sleep too. But the couple of thousands of dollars a week I've been making with the Underground is a nice addition to my $15 per hour salary cleaning at Metrotown. Now, if our union rep could get us better medical benefits, then I might be set for good.

A few weeks later, we found Henry's corpse in an empty house. It was the worst sight I had ever seen in my life and I hardly knew the guy. Lorna was on the phone a lot that night. She wanted to know what happened and why Henry was killed. Eliminating assassins is not entirely surprising for the Underground, but it's different when you know the guy.

I could hear Joy sniffle as we wrapped the body in plastic, while Steve was not his usual chatty self. Like most of our jobs, I hopped on with Lorna for a ride back to Coquitlam to get rid of the bodies. I saw her eyes get misty, and mine did too.

"I guess there are nights like these," I said, breaking the eerie silence.

"Yeah, but you know work is work, right?"

"Does it have to be?"

Lorna's silence made me feel as if I had overstepped some boundaries.

I helped her unload Henry at the transfer station, and then it was a quick fifteen-minute drive home from there.

Lorna gave me a *sampaguita*-scented air freshener as I hopped out of the van. It looked identical to the one she had used at the Coal Harbour job.

"Do you want to know why they killed him?"

"Maybe it's better if I don't."

"We try our best. Even if the world around us doesn't do the same, the least I can do is be professional."

I didn't really know what to say back to her, so I just nodded. She cracked a faint and tired smile, then said good night.

I placed the air freshener on top of a cabinet and it slowly breathed new life in my room.

I set my alarm for eight and the bright light of my phone illuminated the bloodstains on my hands. I willed myself to get up and wash my hands again with the pomegranate-scented soap that I got after the Coal Harbour job. I knew the stains remained under my fingernails, but the scent of *sampaguita* overpowered the room. I slept like a baby that night.

NOT ALL BEARS DRINK MEAD

VINCENT TERNIDA

Every so often, Mang Kanor had the same dream. He chased his son Kit but never caught up. A grizzly would block his path and eviscerate the boy. The grizzly always ignored Mang Kanor but the boy would always die lying in a pool of his own blood and gore. Darkness would follow and he would wake.

Wednesday morning began with the aroma of beef *tapa* and fried eggs. Stirring from his shallow slumber, the lanky middle-aged man slowly awoke and sat on the edge of his IKEA twin bed. Week-old sweat smell seeped into the fabric. Mang Kanor reckoned it was time to launder his sheets. He changed his mind as soon as he staggered towards his beat-down smartphone. It was already 8:12.

Irish Ferreira, a spunky nineteen-year-old, finely minced garlic in the kitchen. Her bifocals and kinky hair tied in a ponytail gave her a nerdy look. Mang Kanor entered and pulled a wobbly IKEA chair towards him, stepping on it to reach his cupboard. Irish beamed at him with her perfect teeth: the result of years of painful braces.

Still groggy, he took some coffee filters and scooped some Maxwell

House grounds cheaply bought from Costco. He loaded it into the second-hand Black and Decker coffee maker, found at a nearby dumpster about three years back. It still worked like a charm.

"Well good morning to you too!" Irish pouted. She definitely looked a lot like her mother, Ligaya, from a lifetime ago.

He watched the coffee brew and as soon as the coffee finished brewing, he poured it into his favourite IKEA mug and took a long sip.

"Does your dad even know you're here?"

"He doesn't care."

"What about your mom?"

Irish silently transferred the finished beef tapa and eggs into a plate and got a new skillet ready. She added canola oil and waited for the pan to heat up.

"Irish?"

"She's at work and I'm a grown woman, I do what I want."

"You still live with your parents. Until you pay rent, you gotta do what your parents say. It's part of the rules."

"I don't care, I have a job, I pay my taxes, I'm an adult," Irish said as she sautéed garlic. "Besides, I like cooking for you."

"Thank you."

"Found a job yet?"

"Still looking."

Mang Kanor was laid off from his supermarket job two years earlier. He got by with odd jobs, seasonal contracts, and random offers from Craigslist. He made ends meet but with the rising costs of city living, he missed the steady paycheck. He thought about Kit, now living with his mother Luz and her new husband Renato.

"Okay, it's ready!"

"Don't you ever eat at home?"

"Mom never cooks anymore, she's always pulling overtime. And Dad likes his Timmy's too much."

"Figures," Mang Kanor said taking another sip. "Coffee?"

"Really? I work at a Starbucks."

~

Mang Kanor pulled into the Lougheed Town Center parking lot forty-minutes from his rented basement suite near Vancouver General Hospital. On his Sonora tape deck played Six Cycle Mind's *Sige*. The alternative rock tunes reminded him about drunk times with friends. He lit a reefer.

As he hotboxed in the truck, a sharp knock startled him.

Adam, a five-five Scotsman with a full beard, was outside. He wore a baseball cap with mismatched aviators and too much bling. He was the quintessential poser. Mang Kanor reached over to open the door.

"How we doin', MK?" said Adam.

"We good. Hop in."

Adam took a pack of Djarum Blacks and lit a stick.

"Don't you want any of this?" Mang Kanor offered the reefer.

"Not today bro," Adam said. "Let's get this show on the road."

"You got it, boss."

As he pulled out from the parking lot, he observed a young Asian family walking towards their SUV from his rearview mirror. Focusing on the boy, he remembered Kit as a toddler as they walked hand in hand at SM Megamall back in Manila.

~

They first met on Craigslist a year and a half earlier. Adam posted an ad for a budget shaman, but never found anyone in his price range. Thinking that it was a joke, Mang Kanor lied that he was a practicing *albularyo,* a medicine man. Adam said that he could only pay eighty at the time; Mang Kanor requested to throw in meals and gas. When Adam agreed, Mang Kanor panicked. He did extensive internet research to fake the so-called ritual and had their first session around Christmas. He was surprised to land a steady paying gig after that.

A year and a half later, watching Adam morph from human to bear still made Mang Kanor's stomach turn. He was used to deceiving clients about seeing ghosts, but for something tangible as lycanthropy, Mang Kanor could only fake so much. He merely memorized the incantations and movement of runes (which he forged).

When it came to the actual ceremony, Adam would fall into a deep slumber and transform into a bear. As they continued their sessions, Mang Kanor realized he didn't actually need to do anything special. Adam did it on his own and probably just felt he needed the company.

Mang Kanor usually served as a lookout. Even seeing a cub caused most people to panic. To make himself appear more legit, he gave Adam nutrition tips to "keep the bear at bay". When he didn't have Adam as a client, he advertised himself as a spirit medium to earn more money on the side. There was a demand for alternative medicine and other mumbo jumbo. In short, there were tons of customers willing to pay for his bullshit.

~

Adam licked his jam-smeared paws, coated with mashed blackberries collected from the field. He knew that it was a risk to step out into the open since the wood was human territory, but he could not resist the forbidden fruit. He needed another hour to spend in this form so he could

14

function properly as a human for the rest of the week. All that mattered was he indulged his suppressed bestial instincts.

Gunshots. There were three and then a click. Hunters? Impossible, it was against the law to hunt bear in this province. Most likely city slickers letting off steam. It sounded like a rifle. Adam was now full of norephedrine. He lingered in the grass, attempting to get a clear view of the aggressors. His instincts told him to pounce but his human psyche still had a modicum of control.

Climbing towards higher ground, Adam was now in full sight. He knew the risk but he played the bluff with the hunters: his life against a hefty fine, suspension of gun licenses, and probably some prison time for the humans. They spoke of racial conflicts in the human world but that paled in comparison to humans abusing their position at the top of the food chain.

One of the hunters screamed at the bear and made himself appear larger. Adam found him funny. The boy aimed the rifle at Adam and pretended to fire, but the rifle misfired as the powerful recoil curved the butt of the rifle from his shoulder to his forehead. He dropped to the ground with a wound to the head. The other hunters began to panic as they tried to stabilize him.

Adam lumbered away. He would use the last hour for a small nap before reconvening with his Craigslist shaman.

A round four in the afternoon, Mang Kanor woke up to the sounds of gunshots. Three rang through the air. He got up from his comfortable tree and ran over to where Adam was last seen lumbering.

"Where are you, Adam?"

He worried that he picked the wrong spot. For the last few months, the area was abandoned. He worried about losing a favourite client. Adam paid eighty when he called, never stiffed him, and never even questioned his eligibility. Adam even reminded him of Kit, if his son was white, short, and fat as all hell. Both of them loved rap music, video games, and casual sex.

15

Adam, still in bear form, emerged from the blackberry fields covered with berry jam. The bear's gait appeared ataxic, akin to someone being a few drinks in. Mang Kanor took a face towel and wiped off Adam's face and patted him on the head. Adam growled and he backed off.

"You okay, big guy?"

Adam snorted as the odd couple wandered back into the alcove.

~

It usually took an hour for the fur to dissipate and switch back to the Scotsman's body. The snout would recede and the rest of the beast turned back into a man. Since this was the tenth time Mang Kanor oversaw the event, it was an easy eighty bucks, a free meal, and gas. After waking up fully transformed, Adam changed back into his street clothes while Mang Kanor took another toke from his reefer.

Adam handed Mang Kanor an envelope filled with four twenties. He took the money and rolled a fresh joint. The man-bear refused to have one.

"You always smoke one," Mang Kanor said.

"Not feeling it today."

"Suit yourself. Let's get going while there's still light out."

~

Rocko's was a popular diner in Mission. They waited with a group of teenage townies thirsty for milkshakes. The group of five looked like Archie, Jughead, Reggie, Betty, and Veronica from the comics. The snow blonde waitress approached Mang Kanor and flirtatiously flipped through her waitlist. Her name tag read 'Missy'.

"You boys mind sitting at the bar?"

"No ma'am, we would love the bar!"

Adam rolled his eyes at Mang Kanor's eagerness. Archie and the gang watched the pair get seated with contempt. Archie called the waitress.

"We've been waiting here thirty minutes, you said fifteen."

"Honey, we gave out estimates, we can't just go kicking out guests. Don't worry, dear. Once you get a seat, you can stay as long as you like."

"You bet we will!"

Missy attended to Adam and Mang Kanor.

"Hey boys, the usual?"

"Sure, and the bear will have his mead."

Missy chuckled almost on cue, like a sitcom character. Adam focused on Missy's wedding ring. After winking at Adam, Missy walked towards the bar.

"Quit it," Adam said.

"All the other bears drink mead."

"Not all bears drink mead."

Missy returned with two draft beers. It was summer so they got Granville Island Hefeweizen.

"Sorry Adam, we're out of salmon lox."

"Can I get a cod burger then?"

"Sure hon, fries or salad?"

"Fries."

"He meant salad," Mang Kanor interjected. "Actually, he'll have the grilled chicken salad, hold the dressing."

Missy grinned. "What are you, his nutritionist?"

"Kid doesn't know what's good for him," Mang Kanor cackled as he took a sip from his beer.

"I'm really getting sick of your bullshit every other month," Adam said.

"Relax kid. I think it'd be stranger if I didn't open my mouth."

"Why can't we just do Burger King next door? It's Whopper Wednesday."

"You know the rules. You can't have too much processed human food after the switch over. You'll get liver damage."

"Right," Adam said. He took a big swig.

"Actually, you're not even allowed a beer but I figured you needed something to take the edge off."

After months of being treated to free bar food, there's no way Mang Kanor would eat at a Burger King. Until Adam decided to actually research what the fuck he really was, Mang Kanor would continue cashing in his eighty bucks, free diner meals, and gas for his truck.

M ang Kanor parked near Adam's bus stop. As Adam disembarked, Mang Kanor leaned over.

"We good for next month?"

"I think I can hold out for a month and a half."

"Good. Stay away from too much red meat and try not to have too much sex."

"Gotcha."

Mang Kanor switched on his Filipino rock and sped away. Besides the man's addiction to THC, his tardiness, and his catcalls— Adam didn't mind the affable shaman. Mang Kanor never cared about Adam's genus— whether his bear form or his human avatar.

He took a Djarum Black from his bag and lit it. At $18 a pack, the kretek was a luxury. The head high soothed him. He tried to stay off the weed: the THC made him more aggressive, it was as if part of his bear form crossed over to his human side. A customer at work complained that he actually growled at them and was slightly more aggressive.

A silver Prius honked. It was Missy. She wore her hair down and a tank top. The forty-something waitress looked like she was in her early thirties, and she appeared gorgeous to the half- ursine.

"Hey stranger," she said. "Didn't know you live 'round these parts."

"I just needed to catch a bus."

"It's probably on the way, I'll give you a lift," Missy offered.

"I don't wanna impose."

"Come on, keep a girl company," she said in a tinny voice.

Adam reluctantly got in.

The National played on the radio. He hated melancholic music. Missy changed the station to an upbeat Janelle Monae track.

"So, you boys had a good hike?"

"We go off-roading actually."

"Wow, interesting. See any bears?"

"No bears," Adam said after a long pause.

"Huh, strange."

Adam noticed Missy not wearing her wedding ring. He turned towards Missy's bare legs. He turned away to stop thinking about what would come next. There was still some bear left in his psyche. He should not have smoked the cigarette and had a beer. Man-made chemicals did a number on his hormones.

"Hey, you okay?"

"I'm just a little tired."

The stretch of road they drove on was empty. The homes that were built in the area were few and far between. Adam felt his bear urges rising, he needed to get out of the car.

"I'm not really married," Missy said. "Going through a bad divorce. Don't tell your buddy, I know he's got a crush on me."

"Secret's safe with me."

Missy smiled.

"You have a girlfriend?"

"I had one, she found someone else."

"Bummer."

Adam spotted a dilapidated house incoming, he decided to get off here.

"I'm actually right over here," Adam said.

Missy pulled over next to a lonely dimly-lit house.

"Wow, you live here?"

"It's not much but rent's cheap."

"I bet. Wouldn't pay five hundred for that, but that's me."

"Thanks for the ride."

"Anytime. Oh hey, do you want my number? I can give you a ride since I live pretty close by."

"That'd be nice," Adam said.

Missy pulled a receipt from her dashboard and wrote down her phone number.

"Call me," she winked and drove away.

Adam crumpled the receipt and tossed it away. He walked the opposite direction of the house. A part of him wanted to accept Missy's invitation. Although he does not know whether that impulse was from his human or bear side.

M ang Kanor sang along to Sugarfree's *Mariposa* on the drive home. Filipino rock kept him alive during his days as a single dad until Luz came for his son and struck a deal to sponsor both him and Kit to Canada. He thought it was a winning ticket to an easy life moving to a first world country, so he easily accepted the deal, after all, he didn't need to financially support the kid. Years of being unemployed in Manila, he still made ends meet with the stipend from Luz and his fraudulent schemes. Besides Adam and his occasional marks, living in Vancouver was hard work and he didn't count on being depressed after being estranged from his son.

He received a call and picked up his phone.

"Kanor," the voice on the other line was grave. Luz.

"Uy Luz, 'musta?"

"It's Kit. He hurt himself while hunting with friends."

"Where is he now?"

"Hospital's at New West."

"On my way."

Mang Kanor stepped on the gas. He hoped his son would be all right. Glimpses of his recurring dream recurred. *Did the grizzly represent Adam? Was that the meaning of the dream?* He prayed that it wasn't so.

THE WINTER SISTER

SYLVIA SANTIAGO & JENNY WONG

*S*he only dreams in black and white, of death and snow. And in the darkest hours, she returns to those final moments. His hair is heavy, brushstrokes frozen against the pale canvas of his skin; the whites of his eyes are crescent moons beneath half-closed lids. Blood, when spilled on a winter's night, hides its crimson under the guise of a lesser sin— fresh ink poured across a backdrop of ivory and silk.

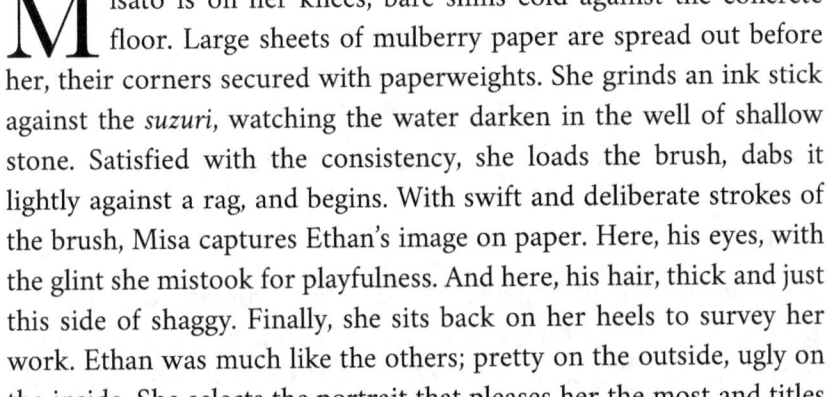

Misato is on her knees, bare shins cold against the concrete floor. Large sheets of mulberry paper are spread out before her, their corners secured with paperweights. She grinds an ink stick against the *suzuri*, watching the water darken in the well of shallow stone. Satisfied with the consistency, she loads the brush, dabs it lightly against a rag, and begins. With swift and deliberate strokes of the brush, Misa captures Ethan's image on paper. Here, his eyes, with the glint she mistook for playfulness. And here, his hair, thick and just this side of shaggy. Finally, she sits back on her heels to survey her work. Ethan was much like the others; pretty on the outside, ugly on the inside. She selects the portrait that pleases her the most and titles it *Yuki no naka, 8.* To finish, she presses her artist's chop into vermillion ink and fixes the seal beneath the title. The characters of her name mark the paper like red scratches. Misa sometimes wonders why she bothers titling and signing these portraits. These are the paintings she will never display, never sell.

She heads to the kitchen for her usual post-painting snack of sweet apple jam on bread. She saws through a hard nub of stale baguette, littering her cracked tile countertop with crumbs.

Her knife dips into the jam jar.

"Rudy-doodie, time for walkies," a nasal voice echoes down the hall outside her door.

Misa freezes, mid-spread, knuckles white.

There is a scrabbling of dog claws on hardwood followed by a cold chorus of clear metal jingles. Bells. That crazy woman in 6C has put a festive harness on her stubby brown sausage dog again.

The knife begins to tremble.

Ever since the Christmas when she was ten, Misa hated the sound of sleigh bells. So perfect and gleaming on the outside, so suffocating and rough on the inside. The little metal clappers tinkling to escape their round silver confines, summoning memories she wished would stay buried.

Rubbing her wrist, she remembers the bruises made by his fingers, round and flat, crushed berries across the pale landscape of her skin. Those were the first wounds he gave Misa when he grabbed her in the alley behind her family's fourplex. She'd dropped the bag of recyclables when the man shoved her into the backseat of a small grey car, its tinted hatchback window curved and sinister-black as a beetle's shell.

He drove like a model citizen: law-abiding, irreproachable. Hands at the ten-and-two position, speedometer needle nosing the speed limit, mirrors adjusted to cover his blind spots. His eyes flicked up into the rearview mirror at regular intervals, watching her. Misa tried not to breathe too deeply or too loudly, tried not to inhale the smells of cold sweat, foil wrappers, and motor oil that had replaced the Ivory soap scent on her skin. Years later, she'd forget his face. It was the eyes she'd remember. That, and the sinking feeling in her belly when she recognized the road signs that pegged the city exit.

When she thinks about the accident, it's mostly in sounds. Her eyes slamming shut the moment the brakes began to squeal. The wheels leaving the hum of the pavement to spin silently in the air. The wailing crunch of metal, the sharp shatter of glass. And in the end, the lone blare of the radio still pushing tunes through slits in the dashboard, a never-ending loop of Christmas carols full of silver bell jingles and guiding stars leading the lost through dark holy nights. Forcing her eyes open, Misa's gaze fell on the stain spreading over her gray fleece hoodie. The seat belt had cut into her belly above her hip bones, leaving a wet strip, dark with blood.

The man was still in the driver's seat, slumped over the wheel. A woman in the passenger's seat hovered over him, her long black hair spilling over her thin white dress.

"Mama," Misa gasped. Each breath pushed against the seat belt, causing a short lash of pain.

"No," the voice was faint and dry, the skitter of leaves across a frozen pond. The woman turned to Misa, obscuring the blood spattered across the dashboard. Her face was beautiful and frail, a dove's feather battered by winter winds. Milky eyes peered into Misa's wide brown ones for a moment, pondering.

"But, I could be your sister," the voice continued, though the woman's thin blue lips never moved. "I could fix what he's done to you. Would you like to be my sister?"

Misa held her breath and nodded. The woman reached over and wiped a tear from Misa's cheek. The small clear drop rested on her slender fingertip and grew thinner and brighter, sharpening into the lace-edged glitter of a perfect snowflake. The woman pressed the small piece of hard cold light into Misa's chest. Misa heaved a sigh as the coolness spread through her body, soothing the heat of her pain. "You will do well, my sister," she heard before falling into the deep empty softness of sleep.

~

The police, when they finally arrived with their cavalry of sirens and flashing lights, assumed that the icy winter roads had caused the man to veer off course. Later at the hospital, Misa never told them that he had swerved to avoid hitting a pale woman standing alone in the middle of the road.

She woke to the cool touch of a palm against her cheek. Her eyelids fluttered, opened, to see her mother leaning over the hospital bed.

"Mama?" She felt tears upon her face; Misa couldn't tell if they were hers or her mother's.

"I'm here," she said as she smoothed the hair across Misa's forehead.

"Am I hurt?" Her hands ranged tentatively across her abdomen. There was pain, but not as much as she was expecting.

"You have some scrapes and bruising," her mother's expression was guarded. "The doctor expected worse from the amount of blood on your clothes."

Misa bit the inside of her cheek, something she did when she was nervous. Something she never did when she was with her mother. Dark eyes, so alike, reflected and searched the other's.

"What is it, Misa?"

After a moment's hesitation, she said, "There was a woman. She helped me."

Her mother inhaled sharply, startling Misa.

"Mama? Who was she?"

"We call her *Yuki Onna.*"

"Snow woman? Like Wonder Woman?"

Her mother laughed gently, though without mirth. She left Misa's bedside to gaze out the window. "She's a spirit of the snow who helps girls and women if she finds them in danger."

Frost laced over the edges of the glass, framing the winter skies beyond. Her mother pressed her fingertips to the windowpane. "Your *Oba-chan* said that *Yuki Onna* came to

her when she was a child."

"Grandma Kazuko saw the snow woman too?"

Without turning from the window, her mother nodded. "She was very young. It was

when her family was moved to the internment camp, the first winter there."

～

*S*now had fallen the night before and Kazuko was eager to play outside. Once she passed the last row of wooden shacks and was out of sight of watchful eyes,

she laughed and began to run towards the woods that bordered the far side of the camp. The laughter caught in her throat when she emerged from the trees. A man stood by the riverbank, a bloodied rabbit hanging limply from his grubby hand.

Kazuko stood frozen with fear as the man approached.

"I oughta do this to you," he hissed, shaking the broken bundle of fur at her.

She found her voice and screamed.

The man lunged.

Kazuko felt her feet leave the ground as he hurled her down the riverbank. She rolled and landed hard on her back at the water's edge. The man stood, looking down at her while she struggled for breath. He never saw the sudden gust of snow that came from behind to smother him, like a swarm of angry bees.

Kazuko's eyelids drifted shut. When she opened them, a woman's face hovered over hers.

The eyes were wrong, they were as white as the rest of the face, but Kazuko was in such pain

there wasn't room left for fear.

"It's fortunate that we have found each other," the woman said. She bent closer, long black hair slithering over her shoulders. The woman pressed her blue-tinged lips to Kazuko's forehead. She felt a shock of cold, as if she'd been thrown into the icy river, that chased the pain from her small body.

"You are strong, little sister," the woman whispered. "Sleep now."

"Your *Oba-chan* told me this story a few months before she died. I thought it was the

medication speaking."

Her mother returned to her, taking Misa's hands in her own, holding them tightly. "*Yuki*

Onna saved your life, for which I'm ever grateful, but now you're beholden to her."

Misa whispered, "I don't understand, Mama."

"You don't need to, Misa-chan," her mother's eyes were sad. "Not yet."

Misa always takes the stairs instead of elevators. She avoids any situation where she could be trapped in close quarters with another person. When she gets to the stairwell, the door is locked.

"For fuck's sake." She gives the handle a futile wrench and turns away in frustration. As she stands contemplating her next move, a door at the end of the hall opens. It's the new guy in 6E. Misa noticed Vic unloading boxes from his jeep a few weeks back, while she was out on her balcony enjoying a post-painting beer. Unable to see his face from a distance, all she could tell was that he was dark-haired, tall, and, from the way he easily handled the boxes, strong. As if he sensed her watching, he looked up. When he raised a hand in greeting, Misa nodded and retreated to her apartment.

A few nights later, she saw him again while watering her pots of lavender on the balcony. He was walking up the street towards the building, talking on his cell. A woman darted across the intersection towards him. Screaming, she struck the phone from his hand. Vic retrieved it from the sidewalk and shouldered past her. The woman followed, snatching at his coat. Suddenly he turned and shoved her against a parked car, hard enough that her impact set off its alarm. After seeing that, Misa had been polite but distant when encountering Vic at the mailboxes or in the building lobby. She wasn't inclined to linger at these times, though it seemed he was.

"The stairwells are closed for repainting," Vic says, pulling his door closed. "There was a notice in the lobby the other day."

"I didn't see it." She tries to remember the last time she left her apartment.

He heads towards the elevator, pauses beside her. "Coming?"

"Nah."

"Claustrophobic?" He looks genuinely curious.

Misa almost wishes he was amused or condescending. It would make what's meant to happen much easier.

"The stairs are faster," she says, fully aware that she's not answering his question.

"It looks like it'll have to be the elevator, if you plan to leave the building tonight."

She shakes her head and starts back to her apartment.

"Misato, wait," Vic catches up to her. "Can I get you anything while I'm out?"

She regards him with something almost like displeasure. "Do you always offer to run errands for strangers?"

"You're not a stranger, we're neighbours." He smiles, "Or maybe saving fair maidens from trips in funky-smelling elevators is my thing."

"That doesn't make you a hero," she replies, her lips thin. Almost a smile. She's about to close the door, but hesitates. "Pad thai. From *Bangkok Curry* down on the corner. You can bring enough for two, if you're interested."

The door clicks and the latches slide in place. Her back is stiff against the door and, for the first time, she is uncomfortable with the rhythm of her heart, the urgent beat that happens when one has been chosen...*him...him. Him.*

"That's a hell of a lot of pad thai," Misa eyes the bulging paper bags Vic sets down on the kitchen counter.

"There's no such thing as too much when it comes to takeout," Vic winks, unpacking the food. "This way, leftovers are guaranteed." Accompanying the requested pad thai are containers of tom yum soup, green curry with chicken, and papaya salad.

"You're just racking up the brownie points," Misa murmurs, laying plates, bowls and cutlery on the clear end of her dining slash work table. A jumble of ink sticks, paint brushes, and rolls of mulberry paper take up most of the space.

"I almost forgot," Vic fishes a bottle of Singha beer from the pocket of his duffel coat and hands it to her.

She accepts it, wrapping her fingers around the ice-cold bottle. "What about you?"

"I don't drink alcohol," he says, shrugging off his coat. "A glass of water would be great."

"You'll need more than a glass with this spread," Misa takes a litre bottle of Fiji Water from the fridge and sets it beside Vic's plate.

They settle at the table and she takes a generous swallow of beer. Sighing with contentment, she says, "How can anyone resist a cold beer?"

"It's cool if people can drink responsibly," Vic replies, wrapping noodles around his fork. "But it's tragic when they can't. Some of the shit I've seen at the clinic is so messed up it would put anyone off alcohol."

"Are you a counsellor?" Misa feels a flicker of admiration, despite herself.

"Outreach nurse," he says, with a rueful smile.

"You must make good money."

"Yeah, but it's almost not worth it," Vic wipes a spot of peanut sauce off the table with his fingertip. "I've moved twice this year to avoid a patient who's fixated on me. She tried to follow me home from the clinic when I first got here."

Misa almost chokes on a spoonful of tom yum as she remembers the screaming woman from a few months back. "Still, at least you get benefits when you work in healthcare."

"You're not wrong," he says, gesturing to her art supplies. "Having a 'normal' job must be easier than being a fancy artist."

She laughs, "I'm far from fancy."

"Is that one of yours?" Vic points his fork at the painting on the wall opposite the kitchen.

Misa nods and tries to ignore the chill travelling slowly up her spine, like fingers of frost grazing her flesh.

He gets up from the table and crosses the room to study the painting. It's a watercolour of Misa's mom, delicately rendered and glowing with pale golds and greens. The portrait shows her in profile seated at the piano, hands neatly folded in her lap. At that point, her mom no longer had the strength to press the keys of her beloved instrument. Misa feels hollowed out

with loss when she thinks of her mother, but reminds herself that it's better this way. Better that her mom isn't around to see what she's become.

"It's beautiful, Misato." Vic turns, his smile faltering at her blank expression. "Are you okay?"

"I'm fine," Misa nods, "I just need some fresh air. Feel like a walk?"

"Want a jacket, or something? It'll be cold out there," Vic says, zipping up his duffel coat for emphasis.

Misa shakes her head. "I'll be fine. This sweater's thick. And I've got an ice chip in my chest."

Vic laughs. Misa doesn't.

The streets are busy as they cover the four blocks to the park. Misa stares at every man that passes, listening, hoping. But the coldness in her heart keeps its silence.

The park is quiet. All around them, the birch trees stand solemn under snowy coats, silent skeletal observers. Only they notice the moment Misa's posture stiffens, the bend and rise of her head. Over the years, Misa's learned not to cry out when the snow spirit returns to share her body.

"Y'know," Vic says as he crunches ahead through the underbrush. "They say these woods are haunted. How cliché is that?"

The snow spirit looks down at Misa's hands. Three small pins of ice have formed in a perfect row across the lines of the palm. With a swift thrust, she shoves them into the base of Vic's skull.

Vic crumples to the ground. Misa has seen it so many times now. A perfect action, as precise as an operation, severing nerves for movement, but not for sensation. Vic would still feel everything that was about to happen, but he wouldn't be able to do anything about it.

"Please, don't," Misa says as they bend down.

"You are my sister, you must heed me," comes the reply.

"Yes, but he's not..."

"Watch."

Vic's body is rolled over, his panicked eyes meet Misa's, but she's not there. Not really. She's a passenger in her own body, a captive in the back seat. The smell of fresh warm blood fills her nostrils as *Yuki Onna* takes her hands and begins to carve her own dark and bloody art.

～

Her body kneels.

They are back home, in the studio. *Yuki Onna* is humming, using Misa's voice to express her happiness. She watches as her hands smooth out the curled edges of mulberry paper, sets down the *suzuri* and ink sticks, and, with gentle fingers, lays out her favourite brushes.

There is a final inhale of cold air that flows up her legs and arms that condenses back into her heart, leaving a warming numbness in its wake.

"Until next time, sister."

Misa collapses forward with a gasp. She savours the control of her own breath, pulling air in and out, her ribs flexing and expanding with life. After a few moments, she settles back, rolling her neck and shoulders, trying to get rid of the remainder of the cold clinging to her stiff muscles.

As she prepares her ink, Vic's face floats to the surface of her mind. Not the usual image she gets afterwards, of when they first met or that initial glint of charm that signals interest, but those last fading moments when he knew and prayed for his end.

Misa reaches out and selects her brush.

The worst of it isn't that he'd died. It's that the last thing he would have seen was a monster wearing her face.

She tries to move forward, to stretch out across the paper and place her first stroke, but she hesitates. Something is off as she stares at the empty space, the distance between bristles and paper, that her hand is no longer willing to cross.

Finally, with a shaky sigh, Misa stands and puts her tools away.

The door closes behind her with a slow creak, leaving the blank paper alone to stare upwards into darkness.

HEIRLOOMS

LILLIAN LU

I wake with smoke in my lungs, warmth coming from within and without.

The old couple is awake, and they're fighting their one-sided fight again. The man, Wei, sits in the middle of the kitchen, inhaling his cigarette and exhaling loud words in their language that I've come to understand. It is the language they only half-used with their children, but the children have left now, leaving the old woman with only these walls of smoke for a shield.

"It's a waste of money," he murmurs. She is turned away from him, stirring his soup. The steam clouds her glasses. I cannot see her eyes. "And how are you going to do it by yourself? The house is fine as it is."

I startle, my bones creaking. I find it funny that he speaks for me.

"It's a waste of money," he repeats.

She closes the coffee-maker and circles around to the sink. I can see her better here, near the window. She spends many hours here during the day, the sounds of the birds outside or the words of the old man accompanying her. I cannot tell if she listens to either of them attentively. She is tired, even though she has had her two cups of coffee already, and breathes, "I will use my own money."

He is silent after that.

Upstairs, in what was once the eldest daughter's childhood bedroom, she has started painting the east wall pink. She has stripped it of its blue wallpaper that they'd kept from the previous people, who'd, in turn, kept it from their predecessors. It has always been young girls living in that room.

That afternoon, she presses the paint-roller against the walls with extra strength. I don't mind. It is the kind of touch that reminds me I am still here.

～

A little girl and her mother arrive a week later, before the smoke fills the kitchen. The mother looks familiar. The old woman calls her "A-Yin," and I realize that it's her eldest daughter. The top of her head has streaks of white and her forehead has some lines, but I have my own creaks and cracks too and am proud of my sway. She still moves in the same manner, with her left foot stepping always more heavily than her right.

The little girl is A-Yin's daughter. Carrie tiptoes everywhere and my bones feel grateful. Perhaps with them here, I can cough away the dust from the basement. Perhaps I can tell her my secrets, tales even A-Yin can't remember.

The old woman brings her daughter and granddaughter up the stairs and to the pink bedroom. Each woman of each generation is two steps away from the other. This is their way. The family before them would embrace and hurtle towards each other with rapid footsteps. The old woman and A-Yin have always been quiet, cautious. When they touch each other, it is just a hand on the shoulder.

In the pink bedroom, the old woman opens the closet and hands A-Yin three plastic bags. These plastic bags have been in the closet for the past half-year. She opens them in front of A-Yin; they are full of jewelry and makeup. The smells waft the air. She hands her granddaughter an old suitcase.

"Thank you, *Popo*," Carrie says, perplexed by the old carpet bag with plastic flowers on it. I haven't noticed that carpet bag in twenty-five years.

The old woman opens the carpet bag for Carrie, and in it are piles of little girl's dresses, all very frilly.

A-Yin clicks her tongue, the way her father does in the mornings as a greeting to the old woman. I freeze. The air halts. Only the dust from the carpet bag swirls up like smoke.

"Mom, you shouldn't use your money on all these gifts. How about doing something for yourself? We are fine," A-Yin says, putting a hand on her mother's thin shoulder.

The old woman simply presses the carpet bag more firmly into Carrie's arms. In English, she says, "Do you like?"

The little girl smiles. "Pink is my favourite colour!"

"I know," the old woman says.

～

The young girl stays for the entire summer. I wake in the mornings to the birds singing and lightened footsteps in my pulse. Even Wei's plodding softens. The only smoke inside is from the soup that the old woman makes. She lets Carrie try a little bit of coffee each morning before her husband comes downstairs.

"You won't tell Mama?" the old woman asks. Her glasses inch up her nose as she smiles.

Carrie giggles and shakes her head.

Their secrets build. In August, when Wei is at work on the weekends, they go on a TV marathon. When Wei's old car rumbles up the driveway, shaking the screen door, the old woman brings their dishes to the kitchen and Carrie turns off the TV, turning back to her books. In those stolen daylight hours, the old woman and Carrie take turns picking one show every half-hour. They do this for hours, almost forgetting about lunch.

With sandwiches in hand one day, Carrie asks, "Popo, why don't you go to work?"

Her grandmother thinks for a moment before saying, "I used to, but then the factory machine fell on my foot. It still hurts to walk."

I now understand why she still grips the railing so hard each morning as she comes down the stairs.

"Maybe when you get better?" Carrie asks, sitting on the floor and tapping her feet together.

Her grandmother speaks so gently I can barely hear her. "Maybe."

The breeze comes in through an open window. The little girl's pink skirt ruffles like one of her grandmother's purple pansy petals.

"Can we go see a movie at the theatre?" the little girl says.

Carrie can't see it, but I can. Her grandmother's brow twitches imperceptibly, a small crack in her façade. "Maybe next time," she says. She reaches out to touch Carrie's hair. She doesn't do this often.

Later, as she is washing dishes and Carrie is writing in her summer diary, the old woman pauses. She turns off the faucet and goes to a drawer next to the spices. She opens it, and I look away. She has secrets that only I know, but she, too, needs privacy.

I know that behind the knives and sauces, she keeps an old pouch of money. I know because when the garbage truck goes by every Monday morning, that drawer shudders and rattles the coins and shuffles the notes around. She sighs and returns to the dishes, scrubbing harder than before.

～

I hear A-Yin's footsteps before I feel them. She comes to pick up her daughter. School will begin in another week, she reminds Carrie.

Once Wei has said his quick goodbyes and retreats into the kitchen, the old woman whisks A-Yin and Carrie up the stairs.

"Not again, Mom," A-Yin whines. She sounds two, not thirty-two.

But yes, again. The old woman opens the closet and shoves something into A-Yin's hands. It is a jade necklace. Then she hands Carrie a red envelope. Carrie knows enough not to open it in front of the giver. But somehow she knows, like I do, that this is all the old woman has left.

A-Yin protests, "Mom—"

"I did not spend money on this necklace," the old woman says in her language. "It was given to me by my mother before I left for America, and now it is yours. For your journey."

"But the *hongbao*..." A-Yin says, gesturing to the red envelope in her daughter's hands. "We cannot take your money." She puts it back in her mother's hands. "Please take it back and take care of yourself. Why do you keep doing this?"

I cannot see the old woman's eyes. Her head is turned toward the ground, the light glinting off her glasses.

Why does she keep doing this?

I feel smoke again. Wei has lit his cigarette. He is on the stool in the kitchen downstairs. The smoke has not reached this room yet.

Carrie looks at the walls. They are her favourite shade of pink. She steps towards her grandmother and the floor-board beneath the old woman creaks with more weight than usual. Their hands touch and Carrie moves slowly, her feet between her grandmother's, her arms around her grandmother's waist. Her grandmother stops, then leans into the embrace, her hands atop the young girl's head, the red enve-

39

lope shaking in her fingers, bent like old wooden beams. A-Yin is not privy to the secret that has been shared silently between her daughter and her mother, but she steps forward too, and puts her hand on top of her mother's, on top of Carrie's head. I turn away, because this is a language that is not mine. It is a language that is not Wei's either.

I do not need to look to feel a ray of sunlight cutting through the room, softened by the dust swimming inside. A cloud passes, and the sunlight inhales, grows, fills the room, no doubt changing the rose colours of the walls to gold. It is fleeting, but warms them still.

A DEBATE OVER THE HOPPING
UNDEAD

URANIA FUNG

Zhao Zhen was kissing his wife Lu Ru when she pulled away from him with a frown.

"What's wrong?"

Lu Ru opened the papered windows of their room on the second floor of the Good Luck Hostel. Above, the moon glowed brightly, illuminating her lovely face and teal silk dress. Below, two human figures reached blindly ahead with pale, mouldy hands as they hopped down the street.

Everyone knew that undead corpses turn too stiff to walk. They can only hop straight, and not very high.

One undead wore a long necklace of pearl beads. The other had no necklace. Each figure wore its hair in a frayed, graying pigtail that bounced with every hop. The disintegrating yellowish squares on both the front and back of their long, black robes were intact enough to mark the robes as the current uniforms of Qing dynasty bureaucrats.

One of the undead headed for a building across from the hostel. Built with ancient wisdom, every doorsill in town was a sturdily bolted

41

wooden plank about one inch thick and half a foot tall. The undead kept hopping against the doorsill. It could try all night and never hop over.

Lu Ru drew back with a sigh. "I feel sorry for them, Zhao Zhen."

Zhao Zhen loved Lu Ru's compassionate nature, but this time, it was misdirected. With a shudder, he turned away from the window and pulled off his robe of yellow linen with black I-Ching hexagrams sewn into it. "What are you talking about?"

"The *jiangshi*," Lu Ru said, pointing at the hopping undead. "They were buried away from home, and they're so homesick they can't rest. Didn't your father train you in the Maoshan tradition? You can guide them back home with your arts."

"You know it's not that simple," Zhao Zhen said. A corpse needed to be buried not only away from home, but also in a plot with perfectly wrong fengshui to become the type of undead corpse called *jiangshi*. That was why seeing one was rare, and two even rarer.

"But when I was growing up in Hunan, so many foreigners had died working there that it was common practice for Maoshan priests to guide *jiangshi* back to their homes."

"I can make talismans for improving businesses, health, and relation-ships. I don't control *jiangshi*." Zhao Zhen took off his black felt cap with its little mirror in the center for repelling evil. "Tomorrow, I want to sell a few more talismans, and then we'll go to Hangzhou and have a good time at West Lake. What do you say?"

He had originally planned to stay in town for a few more days, but seeing the undead convinced him to move on. West Lake was famous for its beautiful stretches of lotus, peach, and plum blossoms among weeping willows. A walk around the huge lake would provide count-less angles from which to appreciate the heavenly landscape. And just in case, there were stairs, zigzag bridges, and plenty of water, all of which *jiangshi* couldn't cross. Lu Ru had asked to go to West Lake before, but now she turned back to the window, her focus on the undead.

"Homesick for eternity. Such a terrible fate..."

Zhao Zhen dropped his cap on a table, shut the papered windows, and placed his hands on Lu Ru's shoulders. "Please, my treasure, let's go to bed. We both need the sleep."

～

After morning sunrays chased the undead back into the ground, the town came alive. People opened their shops, haggled, and led donkeys down the streets. On the first floor of the Good Luck Hostel, Lu Ru ordered a bowl of rice porridge with chunks of yam and ribs. Zhao Zhen ordered two tea eggs.

When a boy brought their order on a wooden tray, Lu Ru asked, "Where do your *jiangshi* come from?"

The boy crinkled his face and quickly moved their order from the tray to their table. "Hangzhou."

He left before Lu Ru could ask anything else.

Lu Ru raised an eyebrow at her husband. "We're planning to go there anyway."

"I am *not* guiding *jiangshi*," Zhao Zhen said, ripping off the brown, cracked shell of a tea egg.

Lu Ru stirred her steaming rice porridge with a spoon. "Talismans haven't brought us much money, but if people can get their deceased relatives back, they would pay much more."

"I've bought you everything you want. What do we need more money for?" Zhao Zhen asked, biting into his egg.

Lu Ru leaned so close to him that he could feel her breath on his ear. "I'm pregnant."

43

Zhao Zhen swallowed. "You mean, you're having a baby?"

Lu Ru rolled her eyes. "No, I'm having a piglet."

Zhao Zhen threw his head back and laughed, not caring that other customers were staring at him. He was going to be a father! He saw himself following in the footsteps of his heroic ancestors—mortals keeping the arts immortal—as he trained his child in the Maoshan secrets that had been proudly passed down his family line.

But he had lost his mother to disease and his father to *jiangshi*. He could easily lose this child to anything. His mind raced as he thought of all the precautions he wanted to take.

He would indeed need more money.

"I—I'll sell more talismans," Zhao Zhen said, searching Lu Ru's face for approval as she ate. "Really, I can't guide *jiangshi*. The business is too dangerous. It killed my father. I was with him when we lost control of the last group. They sucked the life energy out of him."

Lu Ru looked up from her porridge. "Why did you never tell me that? How did you survive?"

Zhao Zhen groaned. He had only been able to stop the *jiangshi* that fateful night because of his virgin piss, which he could no longer produce. No one needed to be told this. Everyone already knew what virgin piss did to *jiangshi*, and no one, not even his wife, needed that much detail about his personal life.

Suddenly, the customers around them quieted, their focus drawn to a plump man in a fine silk robe and trousers who stood in the doorway looking critically around the room. When he waddled toward Zhao Zhen, two huge, bristly chinned bodyguards followed. Their leather vests did nothing to hide their spectacularly muscular chests.

The plump man planted his hands on his hips. "Remember me?"

"Of course. You're Mr. Yang Baobao, the magistrate's brother," Zhao Zhen said, standing up and bowing. "I sold you a talisman for improving relationships yesterday. How are things?"

"That's exactly what I want to talk to you about." Yang Baobao held up a yellow strip of paper upon which Zhao Zhen had written a spell with Yang Baobao's name and birthday woven into it. He crumpled it in his fat fist and threw it in Zhao Zhen's face. "My wife left."

Zhao Zhen had explained to him that talismans could not protect against self-inflicted problems, but the question of what counted as self-infliction could lead to an endless debate that he wasn't in the mood for. He dug into a pocket for his wallet. "I'm sorry my talisman didn't work for you. I'll return your money."

"I don't want the money. I want your wife."

Lu Ru gaped. "No talisman can turn a turtle into a man. No wonder his wife left."

Zhao Zhen warned her against insulting the magistrate's brother with a quick, little shake of his head and faced Yang Baobao. "How about if I double your money back?"

Yang Baobao leaned toward him. "Your wife."

"Try it," Zhao Zhen said, reaching for the knife in his belt.

A bodyguard rammed Zhao Zhen's head against the table. Lu Ru screamed. More blows. Stars and planets swirled before Zhao Zhen's eyes. By the time the heavens cleared, Yang Baobao was swaggering into the street while his bodyguards carried a squirming and cursing Lu Ru.

Watching from a nearby table, an old man told an even older man, "That's the problem with beautiful wives. You can't hang onto them."

"This time Baobao has bullied a priest," the older man wheezed. "Maybe the priest will curse him."

I can't do that without consequences, Zhao Zhen thought as he grabbed a chair and struggled to raise his battered body. Too much pain. He fell on his knees and leaned his forehead against the chair.

All around him, customers shook their heads and made sympathetic noises. A brawny man offered him a tin can of numbing balm. Zhao Zhen grudgingly accepted it.

"I know how you feel," the brawny man said as Zhao Zhen rubbed the balm on his bruises. "I've done woodwork for Baobao, and he never pays me. What can I do? Complain to the magistrate? Baobao's brother won't give me justice. Complain to the prefect? He'll tell me to take my complaint to the magistrate."

"I'll go straight to Yang Baobao. I'll save my wife, even if it kills me."

"It will kill you," a gap-toothed woman said. She set down her chopsticks and leaned toward Zhao Zhen. "Baobao never pays his household servants their full salaries, and his thugs got away with murdering the few who dared to complain to the prefect. They'll get away with killing you too."

Zhao Zhen felt as though the undead were attacking his father all over again. "I can't sit here. I can't lose any more family."

He tried to stand, but the brawny man clapped him on a hurting shoulder, and he fell back down.

"Look at me," the brawny man said. "I've been repainting Baobao's front gate for free, and I'll be going back to finish the job this afternoon. I hate it but staying alive is more important. Know what I mean?"

His household servants, his front gate... Zhao Zhen stilled.

He had been to Yang Baobao's home when he sold him the talisman for improving relationships. Brick walls enclosed the residence. Centred in one wall was the front gate with its pair of wooden doors covered by a tiled roof and locked by sliding sticks of wood. Within the walls, three buildings formed an open square that faced the gate. In that square was a flower garden with stone furniture. No stairs. No zigzag bridges. No water. Only one obstacle stood in the way.

Zhao Zhen handed the tin can back to the brawny man. "Thank you,

46

good brother. While you're repainting his front gate this afternoon, can you do me a favour?"

~

L u Ru stood behind Yang Baobao and massaged his plump shoulders as he sat on a stone bench in his flower garden. Nearby, his two bodyguards were practicing sword routines, and his servants were doing the laundry and sweeping walkways. The servants sometimes sneered at their boss when he wasn't looking, but the bodyguards served him eagerly, so Lu Ru resisted the temptation to choke him.

Yang Baobao rolled his head back and smiled up at Lu Ru. "You were right when you said I could sit here like this all day."

Lu Ru smiled back at him, mostly in disbelief. How could he be foolish enough to believe that she could forget her husband? Luckily, he hadn't forced himself on her yet, but Lu Ru couldn't count on her luck to last much longer. The sky was darkening into deep reds and purples. Fireflies pulsed brightly against a rainbow spread of fragrant blossoms. Servants lit the red lanterns hanging from the eaves of the buildings, and the gate shined in its new glossy coat of rosewood paint.

Lu Ru offered Yang Baobao a third jug of maotai. "So, where's the rest of your family?"

"They live with my brother in the tribunal. It's a vast compound. I'll show you around sometime." Yang Baobao gulped the maotai as though it were water. Three jugs of the strongest liquor in town and the bastard wasn't the least bit drunk. Unbelievable.

"So, why don't you live in the tribunal too?"

Yang Baobao looked uncomfortable as he shifted on the bench. "Why do you care?"

A loud bang at the gate startled everyone. The lanterns hanging near the front doors shook as the banging continued. Servants quietly dropped clothes and brooms and backed up against the doorsills of the three buildings of Yang Baobao's residence.

Yang Baobao tossed his emptied jug and turned to one of his bodyguards. "Song Wairen, tell whoever it is to go away."

Song Wairen marched to the gate as the locking sticks of wood broke. The doors flew open, and the doorsill fell. Bolts rolled. An undead hopped in, its pearl necklace bouncing on its chest. Long, black claws tipped its mouldy fingers. Servants scrambled into the buildings. Doors slammed shut, followed by the sound of moving furniture. Song Wairen had just gripped his sword by the hilt when the undead caught him and clamped its fanged mouth over his nose.

Yang Baobao stood up and backed away. "Ding Hu, get rid of that *jiangshi*!"

The second bodyguard shook all over as he gripped his sword in a white-knuckled hand. The undead dropped Song Wairen's corpse and headed for Yang Baobao and Lu Ru.

Everyone knew that *jiangshi* abhor new life, so they leave the pregnant alone. But now that a *jiangshi* was hopping in her direction, Lu Ru lost faith in common knowledge. She fled for the building behind her and pounded on the door.

"Let me in! Please!" Lu Ru yelled.

Yang Baobao caught up to her and pounded on the door too. "Open up, you worthless rice buckets!"

But the only response was the sound of more furniture being shoved against the doors.

Yang Baobao turned back around. The undead had reached the middle of the garden.

"Ding Hu, what are you doing? Kill that *jiangshi*!"

Ding Hu took a deep breath. He flicked his pigtail behind him and charged. In a metallic flash, mouldy arms flew into a flowerbed. The undead dove at Ding Hu with its fangs. Ding Hu dodged and slashed until he decapitated his attacker. The headless, armless corpse toppled like a wooden statue. Ding Hu cheered. Lu Ru followed warily as Yang Baobao crept forward to get a better look.

Yang Baobao shuddered and waved at the corpse as though he were waving away a fly. "Remove it!"

Ding Hu proudly dragged his trophy toward the front gate, which framed another hopping figure.

Yang Baobao gasped. "Another! Look, you fool!"

Just as the bodyguard dropped the corpse and looked, the second undead, who had no necklace, pounced on him and sank its fanged mouth over his lips. Ding Hu collapsed. The undead faced Yang Baobao, who cowered behind Lu Ru.

"What are you doing?" Lu Ru cried.

They stumbled as each tried to hide behind the other. The undead crashed through a shrub, its musty stink growing. Lu Ru's terror surged to new heights. She shoved Yang Baobao's plushy bulk in front of her.

Sizzling.

Something smelled intensely foul.

Lu Ru peered around Yang Baobao, who was wetting his silk robe and trousers. The undead's mouth went slack, and it fell backward. A cloud of fumes rose up with an overwhelming stench. Lu Ru retched.

In the pink light of the lanterns, Yang Baobao observed the prone figure through the fumes. "Are we safe? What happened?"

Lu Ru frowned. "Yang Baobao…"

"Yes?"

Her gaze moved to the hissing puddle that was eating viciously at the no-longer-hopping undead. "You're a virgin."

Yang Baobao straightened indignantly. "What are you talking about? I'm no—"

"You have to be." Lu Ru pointed at the undead, dissolving in its drenched, tattered clothes. "Only virgin piss does that to *jiangshi*."

Yang Baobao blushed and sank down on the ground. "I've tried hard all my life to be a man. Tried everything. Now all I want is to look like one, but I can't even do that."

He lost himself in a big, pathetic wailing fit that no toddler could rival.

Lu Ru's compassionate side wanted to remind him that his condition had saved his life, but her other side won. She burst into laughter and walked out through the broken gate of his residence, leaving him to the mercy of his servants.

Above, the moon glowed brightly, illuminating the street that ran past the residence. Zhao Zhen sat cross-legged nearby, fiddling with a wrench.

Once he saw Lu Ru, he dropped the wrench and hobbled toward her. "Oh, my treasure, are you all right?" he sobbed, catching her by the shoulders. "I've been so worried about you!"

Lu Ru brushed tears away from her husband's purple, swollen face and looped one of his arms around her neck. "We're going to West Lake."

SCENES FROM THE NIGHT MARKET
ACROSS THE SEA

KWAN-ANN TAN

The market unfurled before our eyes fully formed, similar to a lotus-flower carefully choosing its time to bloom, each movement deliberate and painstakingly carried out. I had never seen something held together by silk and metal move as if it were a living creature, and stared in open wonder at it, which made my friend laugh as she slapped me heartily on the back.

"Close your mouth, or we'll get caught," she said, patting my jaw shut.

We sat on the edge of a cliff, watching the first rush of customers slowly file through the open gates. A melody that tasted like lightly spiced tea floated towards us on the wind, and in one sudden, swift motion, she grabbed my hand and pulled me down the winding cliff path and onto the wooden bridge which led to the entrance of the market. Clusters of lotuses floated beside the bridge, and I marvelled at their ability to grow in the briny sea, as well as the multitude of colours - all pinks and blues, reds and purples.

As we were caught in the crush of bodies that clamoured to be let in, my friend and guide whispered instructions that I only half heard— *keep your head down, let me do the talking—did you bring the gift I told you to?—don't stare too long at anyone, and for goodness sake try not to make eye contact*— because I was too busy looking at the others around me. From the cliff, they resembled other human beings, but when you looked more closely, they took on stranger qualities. Near me, a woman covered a sneeze with one hand, while her other hands held two baskets and balanced a colourful earthenware pot. A man much taller than I pushed his way past us impatiently, his boar head bristling furiously, only to be hissed at by my unforgiving companion and made to retreat to the back of the line.

On the gates were carved the twelve animals of the zodiac, and as we approached, I thought I saw a glint of life in the gems they had for eyes. I wasn't sure, but I could swear that the milky-jade rabbit, guardian of my zodiac sign, lifted its head and winked solemnly at me.

"Keep walking," she told me, a hand on the small of my back. "If we're lucky—"

Stop.

I hadn't heard a voice, but it echoed in my head and nearly brought me to my knees. My head swivelled round in a frantic search for my friend, frozen to the spot as other patrons milled around me, ignoring the fact that I was standing stock-still in the middle of the entrance.

"Well, we couldn't get past them, but we tried," she shrugged. "Get the gift ready."

A blue haze that obscured everything else descended, and two horned demons towered over us as my body shook with fear. My friend looked bored, crossing her arms and waiting patiently as they made their way towards us, one a violent shade of red with yellow sapphire eyes that shone with the light of the sun, and the other green with red eyes that foretold disaster. I bowed my head, unwilling to let them see my face, and they came to a halt before us.

"You know the rules, *trickster*. No humans can pass the border of the night market and there are no exceptions."

"We all know that if that were true, there would be no one left to provide offerings to you, since no mortal would know that you existed otherwise," my friend scoffed. "Name your price."

"Our only price is his life," the red demon hissed.

She reached carelessly into my pocket and pulled out a string of milk teeth that she had carefully knotted the day before with red string dipped into holy water, making sure all twenty of them were equal lengths apart and tied off with a circlet. Now, she flung them up into the air as if they were disposable, letting the teeth dangle from her fingers.

"What about these?" She tossed them at the green demon, who caught it with a taloned hand. "That's far more than you two deserve anyway. You can split it perfectly, I don't care how you do it."

The demons looked at each other and seemed to come together in perfect accord.

"Fine," they backed off slowly, and I watched them retreat, finally gathering the courage to stand up again. The red demon pointed a sharpened claw at me, and I shrank back slightly, not expecting to be addressed directly. "You're lucky the water goddess likes you."

As if in response to that remark, the sea around the market roared up on both sides, froth spitting upwards resembling a cloud of fireworks. The sea's impromptu celebration cleared the blue mist, and then we were standing in front of the entrance again, the crowd noticeably thinner.

"Come on," she grinned and pulled me to my feet, as if the whole exchange had never taken place at all. "Let's go."

∽

When we stepped over the threshold, bright sparks spun and flickered. My eyes struggled to catch up with everything. The road before us was full of vendors under brightly coloured signs, calling out their wares and trying to attract our attention. Our surroundings resembled a normal market at home but was larger and much stranger. Nine golden orbs hovered overhead, lighting everything softly. I felt as if I could spend days trawling through the stalls and yet would never be able to fully plunder its depths.

Bright red lanterns swung carelessly in the sea breeze, and I was suddenly accosted by a gaggle of flying, cherubic creatures who clamoured for me to look at their baskets full of goods - fruits as lustrous and glossy as pearls, and vegetables that gleamed like dim stars under the swaying lights. My fingers reached hesitantly for them before my friend pulled me away, waving irritably at the winged things.

"Don't even think about touching those," she warned me. "They come with a price far higher than you are willing to pay."

Competing scents of spices and sweets wafted through the air as she led us to a walkway further to the left. As we moved past a multitude of stalls, I caught sight of a deathly pale woman ladling ox-blood soup into plastic containers for take-out, licking her elongated canines as she taste-tested the soup bubbling away merrily in her iron pot. At another stall, a pleasant-looking, rotund man dressed in a golden robe folded dumplings— his hands a blur of flesh and dumpling skin—but still managed to gossip with his customers as if his hands were no longer part of his body.

One stall we passed was larger than the others and completely dedicated to large vats of potions. An iridescent steam rose from them and wafted through the crowds as it thinned into nothingness. I peered curiously into some of the cauldrons as my friend paused to exchange a few friendly words and buy some potions from the woman in white-silk robes running the stall, but I only saw my own reflection in the depths of the clear pools. Suddenly, I was filled with an irresistible urge to dip both my hands into the substance and taste some of it.

"I wouldn't do that if I were you," the woman my friend was speaking to said quietly, but firmly, causing me to take a guilty step back. "Not unless you want to completely wipe out your memories of the past two years."

"This is Lady Meng," my friend introduced her to me, "And my lady, this is just a friend of mine I'm showing around."

The lady gently lifted my chin and stared directly into my face. Hers seemed blurred at the edges, the only impression I managed to get was that she seemed to have a nice smile. The longer she stared at me, the more at peace I felt.

"I look forward to seeing you again," she said. "But don't make our meeting too soon."

When we left, I asked my friend who she was. "She is also known as Lady Memory," my friend said. "We must all pass through her in the end. But on special market days like this, she comes to give relief to those who need it the most."

Her explanation and the peaceful calm I felt from the previous stall immediately brought me back to the time we first met while huddling under a crowded bus stop, my small, twelve-year-old self hesitantly extending an umbrella to shield her from the cold and unforgiving rain. Later that same afternoon, I walked back to my house to find out that she was my new neighbour, and that my parents behaved as if they already knew her.

"Am I going crazy?" I asked her, five days after our initial meeting, in the dimly light hallway of our apartment complex. "I don't remember meeting you at all before that rainy day, but my parents seem to have known you for years, and they don't even trust some people we've known for ages."

"Crazy isn't a term we use in my world," she laughed, reaching a hand out to help me with my heavy schoolbag. "We call it fate."

"You're not a normal human, are you?" I said, relinquishing my bag reluctantly. "Are you going to eat me?"

She laughed again, and I wondered if it was really such a silly question to ask.

"I wonder what it says about humans that the children I encounter always

ask this question," she said. "You all seem to live in holy terror of being consumed."

It all seemed too coincidental, but we slowly became the closest of friends for the next few years. She acted like an older sister of sorts as I grew from my gawky adolescence to my last year of high school, providing refuge and tea from the trials of growing up or petty fights with my parents, and a window into another world.

We wandered over to another few stalls. A multi-headed serpent selling demon-warding charms embedded into flaky, melt-in-your-mouth pastries, a husband and wife duo frying up a literal oil storm of sesame-coated fried dough, another canine-headed being selling lavish skewers of barbecued meat coated in a special sauce, and Chang'e, who had floated back down from the moon to sell sugar-spun rabbits that hopped in the centre of your palm and left a warm, ticklish sensation in your stomach.

I was full to bursting when we reached the end of the rows of stalls and eager to know what lay beyond a red, tasselled curtain that separated us from the market beyond. A golden-haired monkey with a circlet darted between stalls. The shopkeepers shooed him away, and as if for a final flourish, he brazenly stole a peach and then turned to wink directly at me, disappearing behind the red curtain before the fruit vendor realized it had been taken.

I parted the curtain at the urging of my friend, and we were immediately greeted by the click-clack of mahjong tiles from the games parlour on the left, a vast space of deep, velvety green, all in stark contrast to the hubbub of the previous food stalls, but no less busy. More children roamed around, playing traditional childhood games with a magical twist, levitating footballs and arrows that shot mini fireworks when they hit their targets, filling the air with small sparks and colourful explosions. Large bubbles, some which contained children, drifted languidly across the grass, where the little ones chased each other through the air.

We watched quietly from the side of a game and laughed when a nimble fish in the pool stuck its head out at the infuriated player to blow a self-satisfied raspberry and dive back into the water quickly as an irritated swipe of a fishing net came its way.

Walking past a child doing aerial somersaults in a bubble to the stunned awe of their other friends, I locked eyes with a girl who looked as distinctly out of place in the entire scene as I felt, her face filled with a glowing excitement. The distinct difference between us was that she was holding the hand of another girl with scaly-turquoise skin, dark hair billowing around her like the sail of a ship. She smiled knowingly at me, but when her companion caught sight of me, she hissed and tugged her partner away decisively.

Growing tired of walking, my friend and I sat on a nearby bench to people-watch. She pointed out creatures and people that belonged to the fairytales of my youth, but fit so perfectly in this surreal place. We watched as Long Mu, the mother who raised five dragons on her own, crossed through the red curtain with an ease that did not match up to her snowy white hair and aged but firm skin. She was flanked by all five of her sons, who were each clothed splendidly in the bright colours of their human form, bickering good-naturedly amongst themselves while keeping a close eye on their mother. The monkey, Sun Wukong, appeared again, this time juggling a bunch of fireworks to impress some children, casually flicking one our way and making my companion direct it away with a flick of her fingers. He laughed, giving a mock-salute to us by way of apology.

A few other humans passed through, each accompanied by a creature of this world, and our eyes met in silent acknowledgement. Mean-while, people stopped by to pay their respects to my companion, and I tried to puzzle out who she was. She seemed powerful enough to stop Sun Wukong's simple tricks, but needed to bribe the doorway guardians to let me pass—yet many seemed to bow their heads respectfully to her, while she merely nodded perfunctorily in response. In the past, when I had realized that she was not entirely human, I had begged her to tell me what sort of magical creature she was, but she remained tight-lipped, as though I were merely a child who was asking too many questions.

Walking further along, there were stalls that held magical items for sale. I gaped in awe at a demonstration of clothes that functioned like invisibility cloaks and watched weaver girls with multiple pairs of arms sew lucky charms and amulets for sweet dreams into clothing. There were even jars that held dancing mirages and shopkeepers who promised that they could make laughing miniatures of loved ones with a single hair from their heads. When my friend wasn't looking, I bought a golden bracelet with red beads for her as a surprise present, one that the peddler assured me would bring good luck, and tucked it carefully into my back pocket.

Soon, we made our way to a stall that advertised a lucky dip, and she flipped a coin to the owner and invited me to dip my hand in and pull out a prize.

I stuck my hand cautiously into the nondescript brown bag, slightly afraid of what I might feel inside it. My searching hand brushed past something that was furry and warm, and I instinctively clutched onto it and drew it out, much to the dismay of the owner, who claimed that my companion had used tricks to get the outcome she wanted. She shrugged and said that it was his fault for putting such precious prizes in the bag in the first place.

Only when we were out of reach of the fuming stall-owner did I take a closer look at the sleepy bundle of fur in my hands, slowly brushing down the fur until a pair of beady, bright little eyes met mine, and a muzzle and wet little nose appeared. It seemed to be a very small dog of some kind, and I fell in love instantly, snuggling it against my face as it peppered me with tiny wet licks of its tongue.

"That's a mini guardian lion," my friend smiled, looking pleased with the way I was getting along with my new pet. "Only around a hundred were ever bred, and they are very loyal companions, as long as you treat them well. The bigger ones are the stuff of nightmares, but this could easily pass as a small dog in the mortal world. I'd heard rumours that his stall was hiding one as a 'prize', to evade the authorities, but I knew your luck and kindness would be able to draw it out. If we hadn't saved it, it might have ended up on the black market, guarding all kinds of malicious things."

"It doesn't look very fierce to me," I joked, still holding the lion up to my face. "But I would love it anyway, guardian lion or not."

"That's what I like about you," she looked at me with a strange sort of longing in her face, but didn't finish her train of thought, and instead looked away to conjure a small basket complete with a soft cushion for my pet.

The next section we walked into seemed suspended in time by a quality of quiet reverence, incense whirling in soft, curling eddies around those knelt in prayer at red and gold shrines, temples spread before us in columns and gilt-leaf, statues of all shapes and sizes elevated above the earth like they were trying to grow towards the star-studded night sky. Everything seemed arranged haphazardly and organically like a maze that had sprouted out of nowhere, the paths uncertain, but surprises and small pedestals to nearly-forgotten deities waiting in unfamiliar corners.

A low, layered chant hovered at the back of our minds reminiscent of a constantly present after-thought as we weaved our way through a giant statue of Guan Yin, the goddess of compassion and mercy, past her devotees laying lotus flowers and offerings of food at her feet and bowing their heads in silent prayer. We were careful not to step on several other smaller altars. They seemed derelict and abandoned in comparison, to the giant statues surrounding them. Flowers and tall weeds ran wild across them, making them seem colourful regardless of their emptiness.

"Some of these deities no longer exist," my friend explained in a respectful undertone. "That's just how it is when no humans pray to you any longer. The temples are a physical representation of our spiritual currency— this is where those who toe the line between divine and mortal pray, and some even have their own altars set up here. I'm sure you've guessed that the larger the temple, the more revered you are in the human world."

A large, ostentatious monkey statue towered over everyone in the distance, and from where we were, I could see Sun Wukong again, lounging on top of the statue's head and enjoying the myriad offerings left at his feet. I shook my head and smiled, continuing to follow my friend as she led me to a clearing filled with trees, filled with glowing lights of temples hidden within.

"Will I see your temple amidst all these?" I asked jokingly, not really expecting an answer. I was surprised when she nodded and gave a shy smile in response, bringing me through the foliage with an easy grace.

We stopped in front of a well-kept and medium-sized temple, its red roof slightly shabby, but mended carefully with gold and silver paper. Small offerings were placed there— gilded clothes and a varied assortment of sweets. My friend reached down and peeled apart a red-bean bun, chewing slowly on it as she studied her temple. There were no clues to indicate who or what she was, except a wooden plaque on which the carvings had long faded away.

As if she knew what I was thinking, she knelt down to pack up her offerings while giving me the answer that I had craved for so long. "After a hundred years, fox spirits can change themselves into whatever human form they wish, and if they manage to live to a thousand years, they can take their rightful places within the heavens as celestial spirits.

"Let's just say, I only have a hundred years more until I turn a thousand, and I have long preferred this form over any other. Over the years I have acted as a guardian and protector of so many children, guiding them into adulthood and through life. It hasn't always been easy—I've lost some to powers that were too strong even for me, but I have loved all of them like my own nonetheless."

The weight of her and what she was hit me all at once, this sister-figure who was hundreds of years older than me, but had always listened to my complaints and worries, who must have seen it all hundreds of times but dealt me grace and patience. I owed her so much, but could give her nothing but the bracelet in my pocket. She took it from my fingers and slipped it onto her own wrist.

"Thank you," she said softly. "I love it very much."

I took her hand as if I was a small child again, and she did not let go.

"Let's go. The market will be closing soon, and I promised I would return you to your parents by tomorrow morning in one piece."

We were caught in the crush of people moving out of the market laden with their purchases. A few sleepy kids were propped on comforting parental shoulders, lights dimming to let the stars shine through. Walking up to the spot where we had first watched the market unfurl, I saw the gleaming zodiac doors shut firmly, the animals' twinkling jewelled eyes dulling into darkness.

The market closed up as if it were fingers curling into a palm, the machinations of silk and metal shrinking inwards on itself, the surrounding sea churning around it like a whirlpool, waves swallowing the market wholly and covering us in sea-spray so violent that by the time I lowered my arm it was completely gone. Only a peaceful sea reflected the glittering night sky.

I turned to my friend, who leaned over and kissed me on the forehead quietly, our hands still joined. "Of all the children I have watched grow, you have been my favourite, and I think it is fitting that you are my last."

I opened my mouth to say something in return: how much I cared for her, how much this visit had meant to me, how happy I was to finally know who and what she was— but the last thing I saw was the jingle of her new red and gold bracelet across my face as darkness overtook my vision.

When I woke up, I was back in my own bed at home again, sunlight streaming through the windows and my mother calling me from the living room, with no memory of how I had gotten there in the first place.

～

Half a year later, my prize had grown to the size of a small dog, and was a perfectly behaved pet, despite his stubborn insistence of sleeping at the foot of my bed, no matter how my mother tried to tempt him away with soft cushions and proper dog beds. My next-door neighbour disappeared completely, and when I asked my parents they responded with blank, suspicious faces, saying that the house had been empty for years now, as oblivious as they had been to her arrival.

I was admitted to university after receiving my final high school grades and was flying to a different country in a matter of weeks. The past few months had been a steady stream of packing and saying goodbye to friends as we left the country one by one, and these were the last few moments of quiet with my family I would have before adulthood truly settled in.

I stood in front of the family's ancestral shrine to offer prayers to my ancestors for their blessing, but before I knelt onto our worn cushion, I hesitated and got another bowl of rice to place above the one reserved for my great-grandfather, adding some sweets and side dishes onto the top tier of the small shrine.

I knew that I would never forget the market, but also that I would never see it again. Wherever she was now, I hoped that she was well.

THE HOUSE OF HAGFISH

DERWIN MAK

S HARKS INVADE LAKE ONTARIO DURING SWIMSUIT FASHION SHOOT. Cathy Wong watched her phone in horror as the swimsuit models rushed back to the shore. An unsteady camera zoomed in on the shark fins circling in the water.

A fashion reporter, pressed into duty as a science expert, breathlessly said, "Polar bears have disappeared from Churchill, Manitoba, but sharks have invaded Toronto's waterfront. Global warming has brought another new species here. Bull sharks can live in freshwater like lakes and rivers. They never used to swim up the St. Lawrence River and into Lake Ontario, but now they have made their way here."

Global warming also moved the Summer Fashion Festival to that warm October day. When Cathy was a teenager, she would have bundled up in a sweater and jeans and felt the chill air blow around her. A decade later, she wore a pink off-the-shoulder top and black mini-skirt as she walked into the offices of Seagold Textiles. Cathy walked beside the slime production vats. Her stomach churned from the odour. It smelled like stale sweat. Even after a month of working here, she still hadn't gotten used to the stench.

"When I got a degree in fashion communication, I thought I would be designing ad campaigns for big brands like Givenchy," she said to Greg, the marine biologist. "I never imagined I would sell eel snot to clothing manufacturers."

Greg shook his head and took a deep breath. Like all the scientists, he was used to the smell. "They're not eels. Eels are in class *Actinopterygii*. Hagfish are in class *Myxini*."

"Well, they look like eels, sort of. Slime eels. That's the nickname that the fashion reporters gave to hagfish. It stinks here. Hurry up, let's go to Alfie's room."

They sped past the slime production vats and into a room with a sign reading "ALFIE". Cathy turned on the clean air intake. Posters of clothes hung on the walls. Another wall had a counter, sink, and refrigerator. Off to the side, a fish tank held a grey hagfish. It slithered at the bottom of the tank like its ancestors at the bottom of the ocean.

The hagfish stopped evolving three hundred million years ago. It has a skull but no spine. It has no jaw but has a mouth with rows of sharp teeth for tearing apart dead fish for food. Its primitive eyes are white spots that lack irises and pupils; they are merely retinas that can detect light but cannot create detailed images. It is seemingly ill-suited to thrive in an ocean full of large predators with vertebrae and good eyesight. It did, however, gain one evolutionary advantage. A hagfish is covered with glands that eject mucous. Combined with water, the mucous expands and creates a thick, white slime that clogs the gills and mouths of predators. Any big fish that tries to bite a hagfish will suffocate on the goo.

The mucous contains long threads of protein, a hundred times thinner than human hair but ten times stronger than nylon. In 2012, biologists at the University of Guelph extracted the protein threads and spun them into fibres. Eventually, the textiles industry used hagfish slime to create alternatives to petroleum-based materials like polyester.

Most slime production companies had a giant aquarium full of hagfish. Seagold Textiles went two steps further; it genetically modified a hagfish that could create twice the amount of mucous. Then it used that hagfish's DNA to genetically modify a bacterium to create the mucous. The vats were full of bacteria, not hagfish. It was cheaper to keep bacteria than hagfish, giving Seagold a financial advantage. Not all companies had the talent to develop and patent a process and creature like Seagold's.

"Good morning, Alfie," Cathy said to the hagfish in the tank.

"The guys want to take him to the fashion show today," Greg said. "I'm getting the portable aquarium ready."

"Whoa. You're taking Alfie to the fashion show?"

"Why not? We owe our company's profits to his DNA. We made him. He's our pride and joy."

Cathy looked at the posters. They showed models in cheap, ordinary blouses and pants. Each poster also had a portrait of Alfie, with his white eyes and gaping mouth. He was anything but cute.

"Now that I'm in charge of promotion, I'm going to change our image," Cathy declared. "Our only customers are cheap clothing factories in China."

"Nothing wrong with the Chinese market." Greg shrugged. "I'm wearing their clothes right now."

Cathy looked at Greg's lime green T-shirt and faded red denim pants. She nodded and silently noted how differently people dressed here compared to her previous employer of two months, the fashion magazine *Tease*. Everyone there wore stylish clothes.

"China is a huge market, and it's great for us, but I want to expand our customer base," Cathy said. "I've invited Dior, Chanel, Versace, Armani, Givenchy, and Gucci to our show. I want the high-end designers to stop thinking of hagfish as ugly and disgusting."

"But hagfish *are* ugly and disgusting."

"All the more reason to keep Alfie away. Let the textiles sell themselves without their DNA donor slithering nearby."

Greg shrugged. "Hey, Alfie, our marketing director thinks you're too ugly to slither down the runway. What do you think?"

Alfie stared up at him with his white eyespots.

"Oh, you're more interested in lunch," Greg said. He opened a refrigerator, took out a dead fish, and dropped it into the tank.

Alfie's teeth tore a hole in the fish. He burrowed inside it and began eating the fish from the inside out.

"We don't need to show *that* at the Summer Fashion Festival," said Cathy.

"Too late," Greg said. "His mealtime video has already gone viral."

Cathy sighed and tapped on her phone. A photo of a blonde woman appeared. "Giselle, the Victoria's Secret supermodel. How about hiring her for our campaign? I heard she came by our booth to look at Alfie last year."

"Yeah, she even held him, but it suddenly rained, and Alfie panicked and slimed all over her."

"Nobody told me about that!" Cathy blurted out.

"Her dress was ruined. It was Alexander McQueen, I think. Oh, is my little Alfie feeling full now?"

Alfie swam out of the fish's carcass. He had reduced it to a bag of skin. Greg reached into the tank to pet the hagfish. Alfie coiled himself at the tank's bottom and suddenly sprang out of the water. Cathy screamed as the hagfish flew in front of her.

"What the hell!" Greg shouted as he caught Alfie in his hands.

"Hagfish can't jump up!"

"I've never seen him do that before." Greg desperately grasped the slippery hagfish.

"When you guys modified his DNA, could you have given him superpowers?"

Greg struggled as Alfie squirmed in his hands. "Superpowers? This isn't a comic book!"

"Then how can he jump out of the water?"

"Well, genetic manipulation sometimes creates unintended effects. Like his ability to live in freshwater."

"Which means he and his offspring can live in our lakes and rivers as well as the ocean," Cathy said.

Greg lowered Alfie back into the fish tank. His hands were covered with white slime. It drooped like a gelatinous sheet.

"Ewww, that's so gross!" Cathy cried.

"You get used to it after a while." He smirked at her. "Do you want to touch it?"

"Uh, no. I don't want to get it on my clothes."

"Come on. You don't have to grab it. Just poke a finger slightly into it."

Cathy touched the slime and recoiled immediately.

"It feels like snot!"

Greg laughed and flung the slime into a garbage pail before he went to a sink and washed his hands.

Cathy rushed to join. As she washed her hands, she said, "Don't let anyone touch Alfie at the fashion show, alright?"

"What's your plan for the Summer Fashion Festival?" Greg asked.

Cathy wiped her hands on a paper towel. "I got some design students to create a variety of outfits and accessories from hagfish textiles. Evening gowns, sundresses, skirts, pantsuits, fall jackets, bikinis, belts, handbags: you name it, the kids made it. These kids will be the Vivienne Westwoods and Ralph Laurens of tomorrow. This time, we're dressing our models in *haute couture*, not mass market. And no more science-y presentations."

"But lots of people attended the presentation at last year's Summer Fashion Festival," Greg protested.

"They were all genetic scientists and marine biologists. We need to reach a new audience."

"That's fine, but did you read the latest email from the boss?"

"Not yet." Cathy pulled her phone out of her bag and read the email:

Cathy,

Using the fashion students' designs is a great idea. Add one more item to your show: bring Alfie along in the portable tank. He's our pride and joy. We want to show off our greatest achievement in applied genetic engineering. Indeed, my friends think I should get a Nobel Prize, LOL. Alfie is always popular with the science journalists.

I know we got some bad press from the fashion magazines last year, but Giselle should have worn the rain poncho that we offered to her.

John Herring, Ph.D., M.Sc., M.A., B.Sc., B.A.

President, Seagold Textiles

Damn. She couldn't get rid of Alfie.

"Little eel, it looks like you'll be going to our fashion show after all."

The Summer Fashion Festival was held at an open-air stage at Harbourfront, Toronto's classy neighbourhood by the northern shore of Lake Ontario. Cathy felt the summer heat on her shoulders as the models and the designers gathered on stage for the finale. Cathy strutted out in a sleeveless blue sundress. One of the design students had made it from hagfish cloth.

Cathy took the microphone and announced, "Ladies and gentlemen, here are the designers of the future using the fabrics of tomorrow!"

Alfie sat in a fish tank atop a trolley cart beside the stage. Greg stood there too, watching the show. Thank goodness Greg had one blue business suit, Cathy thought. It was a no-name brand from a cheap department store, but at least it wasn't jeans and a T-shirt.

After the fashion show, the reporters clustered around Alfie. Much to Cathy's dismay, they ignored the designers. "Hey, can you feed a dead fish to him?" asked a *Toronto Star* fashion writer.

Cathy eased herself between the reporters and Alfie. "Why don't you interview the designers?" she suggested. "They can tell you all about their fashions, all made with hagfish fabric by Seagold Textiles."

The reporters murmured in agreement.

"The designers are at the refreshments table," said Cathy, smiling. "Go help yourself to some coffee and cookies."

Suddenly, a shrill voice shouted, "So this is the creature that slimed Giselle!"

A brunette woman approached them wearing a white silk blouse, leopard print bolero jacket with a matching miniskirt and a wide-brimmed ivory hat, all by Fendi. She carried a miniature poodle in her Louis Vuitton black leather bag. It was Heather von Sator, editor-in-chief of *Tease* and Cathy's boss for two months. Cathy quit *Tease* after von Sator ordered her to hand-wash the blouse that von Sator had worn to the *Vanity Fair* party, the same that blouse she wore now.

"It's got to be hand washed," von Sator insisted at the time. "Look at it! Do you think you can put silk like this into a machine? You should know better."

"I shouldn't be doing personal chores like hand washing your clothes," Cathy had protested.

"I thought you Orientals are supposed to be obedient and hardworking, knowing when to submit to authority. That's why I hired you! You have been a disappointment."

"First, the word isn't Oriental, it's ASIAN," Cathy had shot back. "Second, Asian girls are not submissive, little slaves. You want to meet a real bitch? Meet my mother! And she's Asian too!"

"You must have grown up in Scarborough," von Sator said. She snorted. "No wonder you speak English so well."

Cathy shuddered at the memory.

"Well, if it isn't little Cathy," von Sator said. Her eyebrows and facial muscles barely moved when she talked, a sign that she had been injecting Botox to smooth her wrinkles.

"Hello, Madame von Sator," Cathy muttered. Von Sator insisted that peasants address her with French honorifics.

Von Sator gave Cathy a once over. "Wearing a no-name brand, I see. So you're working for a bunch of geeky marine scientists who harvest snot from eels? To think you aspired to a career in fashion."

The reporters giggled nervously. The little poodle barked. Cathy's heart thumped faster.

"My dress was designed by Miranda Chang from the Ontario College of Art and Design," Cathy said calmly. "We gave hagfish fabric to the best design students in the country and told them --"

"I'm not interested in your no-name dress. I want to see the famous Alfie."

Von Sator pushed aside the reporters as she strutted to the tank. She looked at Alfie and guffawed. "This ugly little thing is Alfie? Do you really think any *couturier* will want to make clothes from eel snot?"

"He's not an eel," Cathy blurted. "Eels are in class *Actinopterygii*. Hagfish are in class *Myxini*."

Von Sator glared at her. "Save the science lecture for *Scientific American*. There's no reason for *Tease* to cover your fashion show. *Tease* is for the woman who appreciates her own beauty and a modern life-style. This eel's slime is fit only to be made into cheap clothes for low-end retailers."

She thumped Alfie's fish tank repeatedly. "See how the pathetic little eel squirms. It's not even good enough to be cut up for sushi."

"Uh, don't bang on the fish tank," Greg warned. "When hagfish feel threatened or stressed, they --"

Alfie jumped out of the tank and spewed his mucous on von Sator. When he fell back into the tank, the splash of water got onto the mucous, and it expanded into slime all over von Sator's face and chest.

The reporters gasped. Von Sator tore an opening for her mouth and screamed. Her dog barked incessantly. Spectators pulled out their cell phones and made videos of von Sator struggling with the slime on her face. Miranda Chang, the designer of Cathy's dress, showed her phone to Cathy.

"My video will go viral," Miranda giggled. "It's already gotten twenty likes in just a minute."

"You PEASANT!" von Sator shrieked. "*Tease* will do EVERYTHING to put your company out of business! You'll NEVER get another JOB in fashion for the REST of your LIFE!"

Madame von Sator stomped away. The reporters and photographers followed her, abandoning Cathy and the design students.

Cosmopolitan's beauty director approached Cathy and whispered, "It was *sooo* fun to watch that cow get slimed!"

"No, it wasn't. Oh my God, I'm ruined!"

"No, we'll be okay," said Greg. "Our company survived Giselle getting slimed last year."

"But Giselle is just a supermodel. Heather von Sator is the bitch empress of fashion publishing. She makes Anna Wintour look like Princess Diana!"

"Who's Anna Wintour?" Greg asked.

Cathy groaned. Why did she turn down the unpaid internship at *Women's Wear Daily*?

A Summer Fashion Festival assistant came by. "Miss Wong, I'm sorry to ask you, but can you and your crew leave soon? We have to get the stage ready for the Armani show."

Cathy led the Seagold staff and the student designers away from the stage. Greg pushed Alfie's trolley cart behind them. They walked beside a beach, recreated in the latest government project. Lots of people, wearing swimsuits in October, stood in the sand at the lake. The crowd babbled excitedly.

"Shark!" someone shouted.

A teenage couple was out in a small inflatable raft. A shark's fin circled them, its head above the water from time to time. The girl swung an oar at the shark's head but missed it. Instead, the oar flew out of her hands and into the water.

"No, no, don't provoke the shark, just leave it alone," Greg yelled.

The boy held an oar and poked at the shark's body.

The shark bumped the raft with its nose. The two teens yelled and screamed as the shark rocked the raft, trying to overturn it.

A lifeguard ran out of her station to look at the shark attack. Some beachgoers called to her. "Marlene!"

"What are you going to do?" Cathy asked as Marlene ran by her.

"We have no protocol for sharks yet," Marlene replied, "but I know I've got to get those kids out of there."

Marlene ran to a rescue boat with an outboard motor. Cathy took off her high heels and chased Marlene through the sand.

The crowd continued to yell; the shark had bumped the raft again.

"The shark's getting aggressive," Cathy said. "What if you or one of the kids falls into the water?"

"It's a risk I have to take," said Marlene.

"I've got an idea," Cathy said. "Do you have a bucket, something you can use to hold water?"

"In my boat."

"Good. I think I have a way to scare the shark away."

Greg pushed and pulled Alfie's trolley cart through the sand to Cathy and Marlene. "What are you thinking?" he asked.

"Let's take Alfie out to sea," Cathy said, looking at the hagfish in the fish tank.

As the rescue boat sped towards the raft, Cathy looked down at the bucket, where Alfie lay curled in water. She doubted the hagfish knew what was going on.

Marlene steered the rescue boat towards the raft. The shark darted at the rescue boat and bumped it. As the boat rocked, Cathy squealed and grabbed the boat's side. Water sloshed out of Alfie's bucket.

"Alfie's already excreting mucous," Greg said. "He must be feeling stressed."

The shark bumped the rescue boat again. Greg groaned as he held Alfie's bucket upright.

"It'll be hard to pull beside the raft if the shark keeps bumping us," Marlene said.

"Not if we make the shark leave," Cathy said.

She and Greg lifted the bucket and poured Alfie into Lake Ontario. The hagfish stayed close to the surface near the rescue boat. Alfie looked up at Cathy. She felt a lump in her throat. She knew Alfie could defend himself, but he was just a little hagfish against a big shark.

The shark rose and opened its jaws over Alfie. The predator's sharp teeth hovered inches away from the hagfish's soft body. Cathy held her breath. Then Alfie ejected slime into the shark's mouth. The slime expanded quickly, oozing into the shark's throat.

"What was that?" Marlene asked, her eyes wide open.

Greg laughed. "The shark just got slimed."

The shark shook its head violently and quickly swam away, leaving a trail of slime in the water.

Marlene threw a rope to the two teens and said, "Tie this to your raft. I'm towing you in."

Greg plunged a hand net into the water. "Come on, Alfie, get in there," he said.

He kept pushing the net in front of Alfie, but the hagfish kept escaping it. Alfie moved too quickly for Greg to catch him. The hagfish dove and disappeared under the waves.

〜

TV news crews awaited them at shore. The reporters focused on Marlene. Cathy wasn't surprised that the reporters gave all their attention to the attractive lifeguard.

"I only drove the boat," Marlene said. "Alfie the hagfish is the real hero. He fought off the shark. You should talk to these two."

The reporters thrust their microphones at Cathy and Greg. Though caught by surprise, Cathy took only a moment to decide what to say.

"Alfie is a hagfish belonging to Seagold Textiles, a leading manufacturer of textiles made from hagfish protein. We are very proud of him," she began.

The story spread quickly. Headlines like "EEL-LIKE FISH SLIMES SHARK" and "FISH WITH NO BACKBONE DEFEATS SHARK WITH SHARP TEETH" appeared in newspapers and websites around the world.

"But he's not a fish," Greg protested.

Cathy laughed. "Let them call him whatever they want. This is the best free publicity ever."

The Australian company Speedo began using hagfish fabrics. Within a month, Speedo had an ad showing a male lifeguard in red swim trunks. Alfie's head appeared in a circle in the corner. The ad read, "Heroes of the Beach." Dior followed next, with Giselle wearing green hagfish leggings at New York Fashion Week. Giselle now cooed that she loved the "hero hagfish."

MTV aired an episode of *House of Style* with guest host Cathy showing the new hagfish collections by Calvin Klein and Vera Wang. Greg appeared as a scientist, saying that hagfish fabric was stronger than nylon. Cathy picked the blue Armani suit and silver Polo Ralph Lauren tie that he wore. He got to keep the clothes but never wore them again.

Not everyone wanted hagfish. *Tease* threatened to give no coverage to any company that used hagfish textiles. The boycott backfired; when *Tease* published an issue with no major designers in it, the magazine's sales plummeted. The advertisers cancelled their ads, and Heather von Sator got fired.

Six months later, Seagold Textiles' sales had tripled, and major designers like Chanel and Versace were using hagfish fabric on their *haute couture* and *prêt-à-porter* collections. Their ad campaigns featured Alfie. Once he was the ugly fish that only science writers noticed. Now he was the new face of fashion.

But nobody knew where he was.

~

"Look at these," Cathy said, pointing to her emails. "The House of Chanel just introduced a hagfish coat for the spring."

"Why do so many fashion designers call themselves 'the House of something'?" Greg asked.

"It sounds impressive, just like 'hero hagfish.'"

"Our Alfie, the hero! All kidding aside, I keep thinking about him. We might have done a bad thing. We put a genetically-modified animal into the wild. He's probably gone up the St. Lawrence River and into the ocean, where he can breed with other hagfish. His children will carry his modified genes. They might be able to live in both seawater and fresh water. If so, they can come to our rivers and lakes. Who knows what they can do, how they'll interact with the other species, how they'll affect the ecosystem or the food chain?"

"Hagfish haven't evolved for three hundred million years. Why start now?"

Ten million years after Alfie entered the Atlantic, the tribe held its annual fashion show, modelling the new clothes they had made from slime proteins. The Chief watched the parade of tubes and capes, all coloured with natural dyes from rare plants discovered in the deepest seabeds.

The Chief did not know that he was descended from a hagfish that land animals had idolized. He did not know that his prehistoric ancestors lacked the complex eyes that he used to see all the vivid colours and shapes. He did not know that his kind were the first sea animals to create artificial objects. He did not know that land animals had unwittingly restarted his species' evolution after three hundred million years of inertia. He didn't even know that land animals had ever existed. The expeditions to the surface had found no evidence of life on land.

However, he knew that he had founded the House of Hagfish.

CAPABLE MAN

BIANCA SAYAN

Lei is stuffing himself with instant noodles that he made with the illicit hot pot we hide under the bed, while *Capable Man* plays on the Huawei propped up in front of us. We're both sitting on his bunk in the ward, an extra sheet draped from the top bunk for a little privacy, relishing the quiet hour after our shift change. On the screen, Capable Man is about to save a little itinerate *nai-nai* cornered by corrupt industrialists on a farm. The theme song soars as Capable Man uses his heightened senses to recognize the danger and his improved reflexes and strength to whisk her away from the farm into the waiting arms of the dependable village police officer. With his square peasant face and modest work shirt, he mirrors all of us, hammering home the show's perennial theme: even the most modest of men can be a hero of *Guo Nei*. Of course, this is deliberate. It wouldn't be state TV if it didn't have a specific agenda.

Lei doesn't really want to watch *Capable Man* with me. He watches it as a fantasy. I watch it as an instructional video for my future. I know it's propaganda for the super-functionary program, meant to persuade people toward becoming *Guo Nei's* own little fleet of state-sponsored superheroes. But there is also an element that deeply resonates with me. The simplicity of the story and Capable Man's innate goodness is a deep comfort that the ability to be a hero is within everyone's reach.

"I want you, again, Lei, to imagine what *Guo Nei* would be like if even one-in-a-thousand of us were like Capable Man, even one-in-ten-thousand! That's why you need to do the program with me. You are a good person. To become Capable is a natural moral extension of being good." The last line is textbook Capable propaganda that I use to tease Lei.

Lei gives me a look.

"Who will save my mother and father from starvation while I'm out saving all of these strangers?" He points his chopsticks at me. He tactfully does not mention my savings for the treatment and the pathetic amounts of money I send back to my parents, my almost middling age when I can get the treatment, the neurological and psychological tests I must pass, the requisite 10,000 hours of training, or the mysterious final selection process. Failing the government-sanctioned route, the perpetual second option of modern *Guo Nei* is to not leave matters up to meritocracy, but money. Meanwhile, the *fu-er-dai* don't bother with the super-functionary program, they simply pay for the overseas clinics. After all, they wouldn't want to be beholden to participating in the super-functionary program.

Someone who didn't know Lei would think that he is some sort of pessimist. I know him well enough to know that he is simply a very practical man.

Me, I want to be Capable Man. We are all supposed to want to be Capable Man.

Lei lunges for the tablet. "Okay, I think we've both had our fill of your hero stuff."

But my bio-chip starts its gentle beeping, reminding me to train before I rest. When I had first moved to Guangdong, I programmed a rejected bio-chip off the assembly line to count down the hours of training until I qualify for the super-functionary program. They glow along the lifelines of my hand, resembling a superstitious affirmation. When my mind is going numb on the assembly line, I check the number and think about what my life might become in so many years. I haven't missed a day in a year and three months. I have even gone so far as to not visit my parents. They're very patient. Most other parents would have laid down their expectations of duty, but my grandfather was a police officer. I think my father understands. It's only natural to want more than to stay home with no work prospects or making the pilgrimage to the city for factory work.

Lei ushers me out of his bunk. He's fussing with his bunk, curling up comfortably, as I head to the rooftop to train in the evening air.

~

Lei is fast asleep when I come back down. Niu has come back from his late shift and is carelessly slumped in his bunk across from mine, asleep in his factory uniform. We used to train together almost every day, but Niu got switched to a different shift for a while, and I could never seem to catch him when he wasn't sleeping or already deep in a game. We got put together randomly in the factory dorm, but we fast developed our own kind of intimacy that makes being so far away from our families and hometowns somewhat bearable. I'm terribly grateful for Lei and Niu.

I know I should go to sleep, but instead I grab the tablet, fiddling with the proxy software so I can get some of the banned American feeds.

Sophia Chau's feed regularly covers unofficial super-functionaries, the very few determined to be a hero with or without government sanction - The Guangdong Prowler, who breaks up bar fights and muggings in the waning hours of the night; and the Serpent of Wuhan, who benevolently escorts women home late at night.

Chau covers even the ones that operate firmly in the grey areas of state morality - the Paring Knife, who takes revenge on behalf of wronged women; the Purple Heron, a cat burglar who steals valuable works from shady businessmen and leaves them in museum offices;

and the Thorn, who regularly leaves dead triad bosses on police station doorsteps.

Tonight she follows Ca Wei Dong, a well-known Capable private investigator in Shanghai, and the triad issues. It pains me to even admit this about *Guo Nei* or Increased Capability, but I've heard much about the triads having Capable members. Members of the Big Circle Gang and the Green Gang have been witnessed publicly doing things only Capable Men can do, showing such flagrant feats of strength and displaying a distinctly invincible swagger.

In the morning, I wake up with the tablet tied up in my sheets and vague dreams of a TV triad villain chasing me through the factory floor aisles.

~

My shift is almost over. I have floated through the last hour, my fingers doing all the hard work by themselves. I've been soldering for two years, and working on the same biochip model for at least eight months. Any other night I would go home, try to stick two or three good hours of training in. Tonight is one of those rare nights that I won't.

Lei and I are going to meet his cousin at a dumpling house between our two manufacturing complexes. I'm not opposed to Ai, quite the opposite in fact. She renders me quite dumb, and so she doesn't have a particularly good opinion of me.

Lei doesn't point his chopsticks at me here as he does at home. He is more of a gentleman. He is trying to ingratiate himself into Ai's room-mate's good graces. Ai is here as a chaperone. I am here to occupy Ai.

They are talking about what everyone in the restaurant is talking about: leaving Guangdong (ideally with a fiancée in tow), going home, and opening some sort of business (no one wants to farm, even with all of its advancements). I don't say much. It's almost a ritual: home-towns, parents, and the pull of the city and home. There is always shrewd speculation about the right store to open back home, and the dismissive talk of a slowing manufacturing sector. *You can't have kids in the city*, someone always says.

I keep quiet. I don't dream of these things. But Ai draws me back in.

"What about you, Fei? Will you go back home?"

"Didn't you know?" Lei puts his hand to his heart in mock shock. "Fei's plan is to become the next Capable Man."

"I don't know anything about Fei," Ai says with just enough good humour to take the sting away. "He is always so quiet."

"I find that very admirable," Ai's roommate speaks up. "It shows you have a good heart, Fei." She smiles shyly. Lei's mocking tone and visage disappear. Biyu has revealed herself to be a secret romantic, like me. Lei's tendency toward heavy cynicism won't help him here. Lei taps his chopsticks gently against his bowl, his secret absent way of saying *there you go, Fei*. I don't think he minds a romantic so much. He is friends with me, after all. And so much cynicism can't be doubled in a relationship. Lei needs to be balanced out. He would argue, I guess, that I do, too.

"Is the process safe, though?" Ai asks, her brow furrowed. "I've heard things from the overseas clinics."

"It's very safe," but I can't deny her claim. The process itself is a jumble of technologies: implants, augmentations, CRISPR switches. One day, I will walk into a clinic with nothing but potential, and they will wave their surgical wands over my body. My transformation will be complete.

"Being a good person is more complicated now," Ai says thoughtfully. "It is not in the moments when you must jump on the tracks to save a woman, but when you have to fix what drove the woman there in the first place. When you are asked to take a bribe, look away when your co-worker is being taken advantage of, assemble an unsafe product, walk by people starving on the street, when you must place yourself in danger." She looks at me with her large eyes, and I immediately know that every single one of those examples are true to her. "It is then that you truly discover how unheroic you are capable of being." It's unnerving but fair.

We go for a walk afterward, the girls pausing at each stand to assess animated cell phone cases and mechanized earrings. Lei and I don't bother. Our weekly funds were all used up for the non-canteen dumpling house.

I am uneased. I don't believe Ai's words to be untrue. But they fall to the ground, waiting for a solution.

It is already late but I won't go to bed without doing at least an hour. The headset boots up for reflex training. My government version has its own tweaks, ethical scenario decision-making laced right in. It always feels like a test to me, but the documentation online tells me that I am given little neuro-electrical nudges, herding me incrementally toward instinctual morality. In more liberal countries, this is considered brainwashing. Maybe they're right, but I guess they would rather be free than good. I guess I'd rather be good. I know that the headset is rewiring me in other ways, making my brain more flexible, more able to integrate with implants, and able to react faster. Sometimes the very essence of bravery to simply be able to act when warranted.

The implant activates and I'm on a generic street corner that could be anywhere in Guangzhou. The randomness of the simulation is important. Eventually, there will be something for me to fix, someone for me to rescue, some horrible thing for me to mitigate. I circle the block, jostling people on the busy sidewalks, waiting for something bad to happen.

～

In the thin crescent of time before bed, I sometimes watch the super-functionary feeds. At any time, I could watch any one of the hundreds of mandatory super-functionary bodycams. Tonight, I watch Dai Duo, a relative novice. Dai is padding through the streets of

Chengdu, looking for trouble. His stats are in the upper-right hand corner; he averages three engagements a night, with not a single fatality yet. Most of his engagements have ended before they escalated at all. The comments say that Dai Duo has a persuasive empathy, a completely different type of super-power.

Tonight seems quiet for him, and I think about shutting the feed off, but then he gets a call from the Chengdu police dispatch. Action is promised. I decide I can afford another 20 minutes without sleep. Dai Duo catches a ride from a passing police car, is dumped unceremoniously outside a residential apartment, and strides up ten flights of stairs where he bursts into an apartment and lunges out the window, grabbing a very surprised *shifu* sitting on the ledge, obviously distraught. They wrestle unceremoniously on the ground.

"Please, *xian sheng*, I'm here to help!"

The old guy tires out and begins crying pitifully. Dai cradles him tenderly. I can see why Dai Duo's feed has become so popular. It's uncomfortable and confusingly gentle. I fall asleep thinking about him, about his good, perceptive heart, and whether I'll ever have a knack similar to his.

Niu has the sheets wrapped around the upper bunk like a curtain. It's his preference to do that when he is using his gaming headset. His training headset hangs on the bedpost for the last few months almost entirely unused.

"Lei, the new *StarEmpire* is sublime. Worth every penny of my savings," he cackles. Lei is very good-natured about listening to Niu extoll the virtues of a new immersive game. I used to play *wuxia*-style gaming before, with noble martial arts heroes, but they prefer grittier, more morally ambiguous American-style games.

"I'm going up to train, Niu. Did you want to come?" I'm getting more and more tentative when I ask.

Niu and Lei look at me, and a sense of discomfort settles between us. Lei looks pointedly at Niu.

"What?"

"I'm not going to train anymore, Fei." Niu's gaze is evasive. An uncomfortable silence blooms between us before Niu crushes it in a rush of words. "I work twelve hours a day. It was a mistake. We never talked about how we would have to give things up. Like, maybe the chance to ever have a family. If we even ever get into the super-functionary program."

I don't know what to say. "Niu…"

"It's not for us anyways." His voice twists. "The cost of the headset, all the time for training, the treatments. These are luxuries, not for working people."

It's not an unfair thing to say. I am years away from my 10,000 hours, but my circumstances are not insurmountable and neither are Niu's.

"We knew that." I falter. "If you've changed your mind, I respect that, but we knew that. You and I had a plan–"

"Well, I can't," he snaps. "When do you plan, exactly, to establish yourself? To win a wife? You think you can work here forever? Maybe meet a girl on the assembly line? Move her into your bunk?"

"No, I—" I'm caught off-guard. I'll admit I haven't always been the most practical person. But I'm not sure there is a point life if it doesn't have to do with becoming better.

"I'm tired, he says heavily. "I can't bear the city. I have to save up enough to go back home. I want to be near my parents. I want to get married someday. I need money for that. You have to forgive me, Fei."

"There is nothing to forgive," I say, but I don't feel it. Who is this man? He used to watch the same super-functionary videos with me. He used to worry about the world with me. It was irrelevant that it was easier for people of greater means, the children of our bosses and bosses' bosses. A truly admirable life was within our reach.

"I don't want to dissuade you." His voice is so cautious.

My throat crumples a little. It's always easier to do something hard when you're not on your own.

I crawl into my bunk. My headset hangs there. I didn't want to train. My stomach is upset and I suddenly feel alone. 4,343 hours. Much more time to go. I carry my gear up the fire stairs to the roof. To the left, there are seven people moving through *Grasp the bird's tail*, framed by the sun. Taiji at its most elegant. To the right, almost invisible, are a couple, the tops of their heads above the HVAC installation in their best effort at a secret liaison.

This time I go through a middleman exercise, training my mind to interact with my body through an electronic middleware. It requires space to move, more than the spacious coffin that is my personal space.

In a soothing harmony, the exercise mirrors the subtle, controlled taiji movements, and I adjust gently to match the flock across the roof. My heart slows, my stomach un-turns, my throat un-constricts. The air isn't the best, but it's better than the dormitory, and I relish it. When I go to bed, I check my watch. 4,341 hours left.

~

Niu and I are perfectly civil. I try to listen attentively to Niu and Lei's in-depth analyses of their guild's raiding strategies for *The Thousand Year War*. I try not to notice when Niu's headset disappears permanently. Lei drags me on two more chaperone dates with Biyu and Ai, so he is suitably distracted with what is unfolding between him and Biyu. As much as anything can unfold whether you're a factory worker.

Ai and Biyu meet us near the Ronggui. The night market is so much stimulation after my perfect circles of factory work and training. We occupy a rickety plastic table near the water so we'll be able to see the illicit pocket cigarette boat racers in their lurid neon. Lei has run off to get a few fried squid sticks and a snow ice.

Maybe because she is nice, maybe because she is interested, Biyu is talking to me about the Increased Capability treatment.

"I sometimes wonder why everyone doesn't try," she says shyly. I do too. Find me a person that hasn't imagined having superpowers. Yet, very few people pursue Increased Capability.

I can't pretend to know why. "Well, we used to be more collectivist."

"Or pretended to be," Ai interjects, but not unkindly.

"In America," Biyu says a bit timidly, "there is so much superhero literature, but I realized it's not like Capable Man. It's just entertainment for them. They don't learn anything from it; it doesn't inspire them to be more heroic at all."

"I always thought it's because no one needs any rescuing over there." We always hear that America is a place filled with people who have nothing to want for. Sometimes I see quite the opposite on the news, that their lives are not more fortunate than mine. But, then, where is their yearning for justice?

Lei has snuck up on us. He speaks with his typical authoritativeness. "Americans are raised differently, you know this. They don't take care of their own."

Sometimes we watch American shows, and it seems that way, and sometimes it doesn't. It's hard to know whether it's truly a bright, hard world where everyone has a swimming pool and no parents to care for.

"I think it really has to do with the commitment. There is no cheating, no getting around it." Ai says. It's true. The brain must be changed and it must be done gradually. It requires dedication: work that cannot be given to someone else. It comes down to 10,000 hours of your life.

Biyu is about to say something, but we get cut off by the roar of a passing boat, and I try to enjoy myself for the night and not look at my telltale hand.

∽

I try not to think about Sophia Chau's recent reporting. More and more, there are stories of the super-functionaries attempting to manage the enhanced *fu-er-dai*, chasing after them like frenzied nannies: preventing car-crashes, stopping fights outside nightclubs, and wrestling them from dangerous ledges. The rhetoric is alarming, that the super-functionaries have turned into government babysitters for important children. The government has also been making use of the super-functionaries for mafia infiltration, just sending them in with no backup, expecting them to manage themselves. The lucky ones are being assigned to guard banks and top-tier government officials. I know I sound naive, but it isn't what I would imagine it to be like. There are no colourful super-villains at our borders or raining from the skies. It's these mundane problems, I suppose, that need to be solved. There are no colourful super-villains at our borders or raining from the skies. I knew that. I know that. I just want it to still be meaningful. Lei feeds me these articles, but I suspect it's Niu prompting him to do so, sending a messenger ahead with the sour news. And still, out of habit or faith, I am still training. Still 4,200 hours to go.

∽

It's after my shift, and I'm feeling particularly tired and lonely. The only thing that will do is to turn into the feeds. Then, I promise myself, I will go up on the rooftop and train for an hour. I check on Dai Duo's feed first, but it's blank, which is not unusual. Even super-functionaries sleep. There's a little notice symbol at the bottom that I've never seen before, and I click on it. Up pops an announcement of Dai Duo's death. Urgently, I look for confirmation outside the feeds and find it. Poor Dai Duo. There is already news on the circumstances of his death, clear in facts, unclear in motive: an anonymous call to the local station, the suggestion of interlopers at opposition party head-quarters, some sort of unknown assailant, some sort of crossfire. But the message boards are already bursting with speculation; a super-functionary sent in without backup into an unknown scenario against unknown assailants who could have likely been party operatives themselves.

"Oh, Dai Duo," I sigh, still careful not to wake my bunkmates. I can't sleep, I can only mourn for a dead man, a bleak future, and a government that doesn't seem to care for either.

~

Lei can tell I'm a little glum lately, and he insists I go out again with him, Ai, and Biyu.

"The problem is you never talk to anyone," he complains. "Your numbers will be there when you get back."

Indeed they will. The foreboding I feel tells me that Lei is at least a little bit right; the numbers are haunting me, and I need a little time to think about something else.

Lei watches approvingly as I put on my good shirt and marches me out of the complex to the Workers Arcade a couple of blocks away.

"I don't think I've been here in... years." I'm gawking. The arcade looks so different. The VR booths look upgraded, and there appears to be an augmented reality obstacle course taking up a whole wall.

"I know."

I make a face at him, but he only makes a face back. "The Americans have a saying about you: *all work makes Fei boring.*"

"I'm fine with being boring," I huff, but he ignores me, for Ai and Biyu have arrived.

Lei is familiar but still gentlemanly. He buys us two beers to split, and we talk about what to try at the arcade. I keep quiet, I have no clue what there is to do there anymore. Ai and Biyu have the opposite problem, they're bursting with excitement from the choices. They magnanimously do not mention any of the love simulations available but also don't mention the blood-and-guts first-person shooters.

"How about *Chi's Destiny*, Fei?" They are suggesting a classic wuxia-style game they know I usually prefer.

"Oh," I'm a little uncomfortable. I don't really want to play a hero. "That's nice, but I don't think I'm up for it. I'm happy to play anything you guys choose."

"Even *Love Potion Witch*?" Biyu teases, but a fluffy love potion game sounds better than anything with fighting or blood.

In the end, we play *New Gods*, standing over *Guo Nei* among the clouds, trying to decide what to do with the country. Will natural disasters happen? Will *Guo Nei* go to war with Kazakhstan? Where would we build new dams across the landscape?

After the game, it's my turn to buy two beers, pouring them among the four cups, while Ai, Lei, and Biyu chatter away. But, eventually, they notice I don't have much to say.

"You're so quiet, Fei." Ai prods.

Lei is kind enough to speak for me. "A super-functionary Fei respected died this week, and he's really taken it to heart."

Ai and Biyu nod sympathetically.

"He was such a good man." I try to explain my melancholy. I don't know this man, but I feel his loss deeply. "He had a special quality, he really seemed to touch everyone he interacted with. He saved people as much with his empathy as with any of his Capability."

Biyu touches my hand, "He sounded like a special person, Fei. You're right to mourn for him. We need more people like him."

"I think so, too." I'm hesitant. "He died in a raid at opposition party offices. I'm a little worried that, maybe, the government isn't doing everything it can. I've been reading things, it does seem like they could be more careful." Lei shakes his head at me; I easily translate it to *no politics, Fei, not everyone likes that,* but Ai is nodding.

"I know you've always been attracted to direct actions, but I do see that the greatest good can be done in the grey areas, where corruption happens. That's what killed this man. I remember when the program started. It seemed to be much more about the people, but the only time I see super-functionaries now is at the elbow of the State Chairperson."

Lei looks at us as if we're aliens. I know Lei has always felt he doesn't have the luxury of debating the ethics of *Guo Nei* when he is so at the mercy of them.

"Why do you always make me regret taking you out with me?" he says jokingly as we leave, but he punches me lightly on the arm and I know he really doesn't mean it.

When I crawl back in my bunk, my old tablet flashes a new episode of *Capable Man* at me, but I still don't have the heart to watch it. There is something ominous about it now.

A nyone on the assembly line will tell you that, given long enough on the same station, one develops a soothing rhythm that allows the mind to leave the body. The manufacturing floor is never silent, but the dull roar, even through shift changes, is a steady constant. Until today, it isn't.

Later on, we would find out the event was precipitated by a weak pin. But in the moment, the signature is a barely-audible howl. I try not to look up, but the howl persists dully. It pierces through my earplugs, possesses my hands. I jam the emergency button timidly, then fervently. But there is no flutter of activity behind me.

My headphones come out. My body takes me toward the sound without even asking for permission. Dreamlike, I move in between the tables, past coworkers in various states of work and distraction. The solvent area lies at the end of the row, and, at the center, a fallen ceiling presser pins someone. At least one arm is swallowed in the presser. Four table mates hover around him, the rest still cowering at their desks. One of the people tugging ineffectually at the monstrous presser is Lei. They can't hear me as I approach, and I have to tug at his shoulder. He turns to me, surprised, grips me back and mouths *it's Niu.*

Niu. The back of his head, unbloodied, is just visible under the presser. The solvent barrel is leaking and pinned underneath him. Soon, it will pool next to the electrical interfaces along the floor. We lose whole precious moments standing there staring. Then, suddenly, I pressed the forbidden evacuation button.

I knock the cleaning rag cart over on to the solvent and then turn to Niu, or, rather, his arm. The work floor has a limited toolset. But the work rag cart has a removable crossbar that I jam beside Niu's arm to use as a lever, frozen in closed mode. Lei is white with anxiety as the presser refuses to yield. Suddenly, the presser rolls back open, spilling Niu to the floor in an increasingly bloody heap. We both stick Niu awkwardly on the rag cart and race to catch up with the stragglers exiting the building.

∼

We're told to wait outside of Boss Geng's office. I don't know whether it's to find out Niu's fate or get fired or something in between. His assistant, pinched-faced and worried, comes to usher me in, clapping the door shut behind me.

"Chau Fei," Boss Geng doesn't look up.

"Sir."

"I hear the fellow from the solvent station is a friend of yours."

The fellow from the solvent station. Boss Geng refuses to even allude to Niu's horrible injury inside factory walls if he can help it. *He wasn't there*, I remind myself, *he didn't see the blood*. And workplace injuries are a managed statistic to Boss Geng. It isn't personal.

"Yes, Sir."

"You'll be glad to know he will be alright. He's lost a hand."

I swallow hard and try not to look sick in front of Boss Geng. Losing a hand isn't alright, it's a life sentence of poverty for a factory worker, for Niu and his parents. But Boss Geng has already moved on.

"Chau, what are the OHS rules on the factory floor?"

"I'm sorry, Sir?"

"Your OHS training, Chau," Boss Geng is starting to sound testy, "what did it instruct you to do in case of equipment failure?"

There is an uncomfortable pause as I try to recall enough of the training I took years ago. "To sound the internal emergency alarm and evacuate."

"Yes, Chau, exactly."

The uncomfortable silence this time is because this is precisely what I did not do.

"Sir, it's only natural for me to-"

"Chau," Boss Geng interrupts, tense. "Do you think I'm some cruel man?"

"No, Sir."

"You were in an area with solvents. You've never had chemical handling training. I could have as easily had two dead bodies instead of two live ones. You think I was willing to sacrifice the other employee or some foolishness like that. We don't send men into a burning building to save anyone. We send firefighters."

"Sir-"

"Not following OHS policy is a fireable offence, is it not?"

"Yes, sir." I'm careful to word things as such to not be perceived as talking back. "In previous incidents, I have behaved according to factory OHS policy. However, this time, it was not clear—" I swallow involuntarily. There is no good way of saying this. "—whether they would be responding." This will be two strikes for admitting that there were previous incidents at all and that the OHS team has failed in some way. Boss Geng is accordingly cross.

"Chau, your station is nowhere near solvents, is it?"

"I would say it's within earshot, Sir."

"But not within your line of sight."

"No, Sir."

He turns abruptly, handling the papers on his desk in a businesslike fashion. He is ignoring me, drawing out the tension, pulling the hammer back ever so further.

"I hear you've been doing Increased Capability training in your time off, Chau."

I can see how it looks. Boss Geng doesn't even need to say out loud that there can be penalties much worse than losing my job for simply disobeying.

"It might look like, Chau, this training causes you to behave in a manner that contradicts OHS policy. In fact, it seems that it has."

I don't say anything. There is nothing that would help.

"Well, Chau, what to do? Ho caused a problem in the first place, you disobeyed factory policies. I'm down at least one man."

"Sir," I am doing my best to humble myself. Lip service isn't enough. People like Boss Geng need to see submission in the depths of one's eyes. "I beg on behalf of Niu. He is a fine employee."

Geng looks away, disinterested. "I'm not uncompassionate, but I don't know what you expect me to do with a man with a missing hand. If

93

you can conjure a solution, fine. If not, I'm inclined to be rid of both of you." He waves me away.

There is nothing left to do but walk home, dig my yuan out from the mattress, and use it to conjure a man with two hands.

~

I go to visit Niu in the hospital. He and Fei are conferring, heads bowed, over his bandaged hand. They look up, and suddenly Lei's eyes are hooded as he gets up to greet me.

"Our dear, Lei. Our hero." There is no irony in his voice. He is intensely grave, the formality reflecting the deep obligation existing between Niu and I. I am frozen at the door, unsure of what to do.

"How are the fingers growing?"

Lei pats me on the back. "Nicely, nicely. You just missed the rewrapping, but the doctor seemed very pleased. After a couple more weeks, Niu should be back to being a ten-digit man, eh? Another couple of weeks of physical therapy, and he'll be back on the line, chugging away."

Niu is holding out his hand. He is addled by some substance or another. The treatment must be still fresh. I am in awe of the health centre: perfect white walls and advanced consoles. I can see Lei is uncomfortable, too. As Niu might have said, it was not built with us in mind. I slip my hand in Niu's good one. His lids are almost closed, his speech slurred, "My capable man. I would never asked, Fei. Never so much." I feel my throat catch, but it's important that Niu embrace my gift to him without carrying it as a burden as well.

Lei says, ever the diplomat, "Ah, you have helped forge Fei. You've given him his origin story."

Niu is impressionable in his drugged state, and he is suddenly content, happy to believe his hand in birthing a narrative we both dreamed about.

"Truly, Fei." But he is still awkward, because what still sits between us is whether I'll ever be a super-functionary. Both of our eyes are burning and it won't do either of us good to see the other cry.

"I hate to rush out," but I am apologizing more to Lei than Niu, who will nod off soon. "My shift..." I shrug helplessly. I have to save up again. It seems almost futile, to start from the bottom again. Can one become a hero in their middle age?

"And your training." Lei points at my hand.

I look at it. The light throbs reassuringly. Only 3,632 hours to go.

THIS OTHER WATER

ANAIS JAY

Another filtration process has been added. Level-Five. Whenever news like this reaches our home, we don't think about what's good for our health. We think about our bank accounts. We review ATM receipts to confirm what's left of our savings. How many gallons of Level-Five water can we afford, and what revisions in our consumption plan do I have to make this time?

I turn off the television and go to our garden. The trees that line our fence provide a canopy of leaves that shield us from the sun.

Kela lies on the ground, dappled with a few spots of light. She breathes steadily, but even in her sleep she clutches the grass. Sometimes I wonder if she never ceases to hear the water beneath the earth, gurgling, calling to her, begging her to be its saviour.

But what can one mermaid do?

She opens her eyes. I hand her a bottle of water. She drinks it and immediately looks refreshed. One of the first things I learned when I took her to land is that she needs to consume five times more water than the average male human.

I started her on 13.5 litres but the moisture in her eyes dried and she suffered from chronic fatigue, compelling me to compute a new amount based on my BMI instead. On summer days like this, we add two more litres to her minimum of eighteen for caution. Her fluid intake, unfortunately, doesn't cancel her intolerance to direct sunlight. Three minutes maximum is her limit, or else she shrivels like a leaf.

I joked once that she must be part vampire, and she retorted that even vampires—*were they even real?*—would be disgusted by the taste of this generation's blood.

"You do not know what untainted water tastes like," she would say. "It is magic on your tongue."

I watch her sit up and wipe a tear from her eye. Five more gulps of water to replace it.

"Another dream from your mothers?" I ask.

"I dreamt of her childhood. I can't choose which of her memories or of those before her play in my sleep. It is the curse of being their last daughter." She folds her legs inwards and picks at her toenail. It's a bad habit of hers whenever in human form, pulling and twisting cracked nails as though unable to accept this part of her anatomy. "I relive their lives in my sleep and it's wearing me out. Imagine thousands of lives stored in your brain because there's no one else left to bear them."

"I would go crazy."

"I just might." She wipes another tear. "Sometimes I wonder what the point of surviving is."

I brush the hair from her face. She is cold, and this assures me that she is healthy. "Hope for the day you can return to the water and replenish it with your kind."

"Are we any closer?"

It hurts me to shake my head. But she knows when I lie, and she says that hurts her more. "They need to filter the water five times now.

That's another hundred pesos per gallon of drink, another fifty pesos for our other needs."

She looks at me, solemnly. "Keeping me alive might just kill the two of us."

I laugh. The creases beside my mouth form, and the skin around my eyes crinkles. She fears I'll die by water contamination; I fear I'll grow old without sending her back to the sea.

❧

Don't run, don't walk. Stay seated as much as possible to avoid breaking a sweat. Most Filipinos consume fruits and vegetables three meals a day. They're a source of water and are therefore valuable. Many grow them in their gardens, and most petty crimes are produce theft. Trespassing, stealing, and—when confrontation happens—sometimes murder.

People shower in the rain. When thunder roars, people stop whatever it is they're doing: typing, talking to customers, playing computer games, arguing with peers. Even the Holy Mass is interrupted. They go outside and tip their heads back to catch a glimpse of lightning. They tick the seconds off until they hear thunder. The fewer the seconds, the closer the thunderstorm is in miles. When a raindrop collides with a human, he or she howls, and then everybody knows. People crowd the streets. They raise their arms and open their mouths. Later, they swallow two packets of salts to prevent poisoning.

There are all kinds of salts now. Some call them little crystals of hope. Those who can't afford properly filtered water buy them to treat their supply. I use treated water for our vegetable and fruit garden, but I don't take a risk with Kela. The one time we tried it, she turned green. The veins in her arms bulged and she couldn't breathe. I poured all our Level-Four water into the tub and let her remain under for days to ensure her good health. She doesn't know that I sometimes drink water treated with salts whenever our filtered supply runs low for her baths.

99

I don't mind. I've determined long ago that her survival is paramount to mine. Humanity has robbed too many creatures of their lives and natural habitat at the peak of our water crisis. If all the good I can do is to save her, I will pursue it at any cost.

I repeat this to myself the next morning as I kiss her goodbye. It prepares my mind for whatever I will have to sacrifice at the onset of Level-Five because, while I do my best for her, what do I really know about mermaids? Even Kela cannot dictate the dos and don'ts of her survival when none of her ancestors have lived more than a couple of days on land.

She squeezes my arm absently before I am out of reach. Soon after letting go, the subtle tapping of keys on her laptop resumes. I look back over my shoulder and appreciate the sight of her hunched over a desk cluttered with open dictionaries.

The translation work comes easily to her; memories of her mothers come with the benefit of remembering the many different languages they learned from years of travel around the world.

The heat outside makes me wince. I shield myself with an umbrella and pace to the village gate, where I pay a tricycle to take me to the bus terminal. The bus ride to the Aquarium takes three hours because of the traffic in SLEX and EDSA. This year's the worst, according to the news. People buy cars for the necessity of air conditioning. Jeepneys and non-air conditioned buses that used to accommodate numbers beyond their capacity can't cut it anymore. People can't afford to sweat. Only those incapable of buying even the cheapest model keep public transport running.

Kela and I almost bought a car, but ultimately we refused to contribute to the already alarming levels of air pollution.

We can't drink, can't breathe. Soon we won't be able to live.

I eat my sandwich in front of the shark tank. Ms. Pinky approaches with her half-eaten sandwich and drops crumbs into the water. I raise my eyebrows at her.

"Oh please, Adam, like that makes any difference." She takes her time chewing before adding that all these animals are going to die anyway. "Once the aquarium shuts down, where do you think they'll go? We can't pour them back into the ocean. Seventy percent of them were born and raised here. I'd love to try and sell them to other aquariums, but they're not doing well enough to take in more."

"We can find investors," I say.

"Don't you think we've tried that?"

"Schools need aquariums. Not everyone has enough money to go abroad to see these creatures in person."

"The government is too busy giving the poor a chance at survival to spare any more thought to animals." Ms. Pinky stares at me for a long time. I pretend not to notice. "Are you really more concerned about them than about finding another job?" she asks.

"My wife will cry herself to death if she learns that we're abandoning these creatures."

"No offence, Adam, but that wife of yours is odd. People talk whenever she's here. There's a strange way she looks at the animals and vice versa. It's almost as if they can communicate. Now, what kind of superpower is that? Telepathy?"

I fold the wrapper four times and slip it into my back pocket. "She grew up near the sea. I met her when she was young. I used to volunteer for those massive cleanup efforts in the provinces, and one day I went too deep and came face-to-face with her mother."

"Her mother was part of the cleanup too?"

"You can say that. She goes to the deepest parts and cleans them. We started talking and she introduced me to Kela. When the pollution reached its peak, I rushed back to the province to find her. Kela was half-dead, living alone without clean water at her disposal. We waited until she recuperated, and then we flew to Manila."

Ms. Pinky scoffs. "So you're some kind of hero."

"Not really," I say.

I stare down at the tank and watch the eight-foot sharks swim, more slowly every day. I imagine Kela swimming with them. Her blue-gold tail expands in the water, and scales embrace her body, making it formidable. Her wet hair turns white, nearly translucent. I picture her looking up at me from the bottom of the tank, and she is not Kela, she is *sirena*. She'll look past me if something shinier and prettier is on a passing person's ears or neck. Her smile appears at the hint of real gold, and she risks surfacing from the water to snatch it.

And then I see her mother.

I step back in surprise and suddenly find myself flailing underwater. The stretch of the diving suit across my body and the weight of the oxygen tank wash me with familiarity. I flash my torch towards the face surfacing from the gloom. The silver scales below her eyes reflect the light. They illuminate the outline of an enormous tail surrounding me.

According to folklore, a *sirena* grows bigger the closer she is to Death, but Death will not claim her until she is a century old. So the two of them meet at the very bottom of the sea, where she would've been too submerged in darkness to know the difference when she dies.

With the death rate of marine animals, though, it didn't surprise me that Kela's mother couldn't last a century.

She opens her mouth to release a scaled figure curled in a ball. The figure unfolds and I see Kela for the first time.

I shine my torch away from her and reach out. Kela advances shyly to meet me. My forefinger hovers in front of her small face. She presses her lips against it, and then bites lightly. Blood swirls in the thick water. We both watch in astonishment as her tail splits and her scales vanish. Her raw human legs kick but do not lead her any closer to the surface for air. I bring her to land and resuscitate her.

The first thing she does when she awakens is to grasp at my oxygen tank, glistening in the sunlight.

She had done the very same thing when I found her half-dead in a *bahay kubo* by the sea roughly three years since we met. I held out my hand and she reached for the two wedding rings around my finger. My dead wife's ring slipped off and she gave me a child-like smile that still believed in salvation.

Ms. Pinky shakes me awake. "Adam! Are you listening to me?"

I touch my hair. I pat my clothes. Everything is dry, and I don't seem to have moved from where I'm standing. "Sorry, I was lost in my thoughts."

Kela warned me about Visits and Visions. They move you back in time and forward into the future, and sometimes you won't know if you're returned to the present.

"Overexposure to a mermaid," she explained to me.

She is in the bathtub when I get home. The end of her tail hangs on the rim, dripping water on the soaked rug. The moonlight seeping from the tiny window catches onto her silver scales.

This water, no matter how well-filtered, has made them look less magical over time. But I would never tell her this.

She props herself up on the other end of the tub and holds out her wedding ring to the light. It reflects in her eyes. Suddenly she jolts and twirls in the water, turning herself to human form. She stares at me first with alarm, and then with annoyance.

"You never make a sound," she says as she returns the ring to her finger.

"You never close the door."

She turns over and her legs disappear, turning into one big tail once more. I take off my clothes and squeeze in beside her. She presses herself to the side to accommodate me. The water overflows, and the sound of it hitting the tiles is the closest we'll get to hear the sea.

"Something happened at work?"

I graze my fingers over the scales on her arms. No more gold – not even a speck. "Yes, something good or bad, it depends on how we take it."

"Did another animal die?"

"Actually, all of them are in danger of dying if the Aquarium closes. I mean, *when* the Aquarium closes and if nobody takes the animals before then."

She props herself up by her elbows. The scales on her neck throb. "Are they going to make sure that somebody will take the animals?"

"They're doing their best."

"That's not enough."

I hold my hand up before she covers her entire body and part of her face in scales. She puts it on like armour, as though making herself impenetrable would also deafen her to anything I say.

"Kela, if we can bring in more people to the Aquarium, then they won't have to close."

"So do you want me to wear a cap and sunblock and pass around flyers in dusty streets?"

"I want *you* in the Aquarium."

The scales on her face recede, and she loses the feral touch in her eyes.

This is the most upset I've seen her since the day she stepped foot in Manila. "You'll make a show of me?"

"They don't know you're a real mermaid. Nobody needs to know you're there for the Level-Five water. We can barely afford Level-Four as it is. We can save you, and we can save the Aquarium and all its animals."

"All its animals," she says, "including me."

Kela remains underwater for the rest of the night. In the morning, I print the proposal while she packs my old scuba diving outfit into her satchel bag.

T he Aquarium brings hope—more importantly, the Aquarium makes money.

She performed in a scuba diving outfit the morning I made my proposal. That was a month ago. Today, she owns an entire wardrobe of tails that she wears above her real one just to keep up the act. She also dyed her hair white to make her underwater transformation undetectable.

I stand with the crowd to watch this magnificent girl swim with sea creatures. As part of the excitement—and secretly as protection against Kela's primal instincts—a huge sign by the door advises people to hide their jewellery or anything shiny.

A gallery outside explains the myth of the *sirena*. It shows inaccurate images of mermaids, some romanticized, some made terrifying by their association with the *litao* and the *aswang*, along with stories of sightings and successful catches.

Kela does her best to master self-control, but every so often, somebody will secretly dangle a silver bracelet to her, and she'll press her nose against the glass to ogle its beauty. She scratches the glass uselessly and earns shrieks from the children and laughter from the adults.

I keep a strict watch on her in case this happens. One push of a button and the huge spotlight on top of the aquarium steals her attention. I wave at her with a variety of gold and silver in my hands, and in seconds, she's at the surface. This trick has never failed, and I pray it never does. It's the only way I can remind her to go up for air so that people don't discover she doesn't need to.

Sometimes, however, Kela loses herself, and I have to dim the lights so that people won't notice the extra scales growing across her abdomen and climbing up to her face. I signal her to rise and she clings to the edge of the tank. She cries about memories of her mothers. Too many Visits from the past, and no more Visions of the future.

"It may be because there is no future, Adam," she says.

Whenever Kela cries, the staff presumes the water hasn't been filtered well enough and is affecting her health. The Aquarium volunteers to pay for her medical needs—she is too valuable to lose now—but we both refuse. She may take on a human form, but she can't assure me that it makes her one through and through. Whatever the doctor finds may only bring us more problems.

I carry her to our car after most shows (we lose our battle against air pollution), and we drive home looking forward to hours in our new bathtub.

Refraction creates the illusion of a bigger tail, I tell myself. Its blue and gold colour has returned, and she tells me that her hair is slowly regaining its health. I kiss her and note that her lips are fuller, her jaws more prominent.

I ignore these changes night after night until her costume designer brings the tears on her fake tails to my attention. She shows me a comparison of her first measurement and her most recent one.

"Kela isn't getting fat." She stretches the tail to emphasize the tears. "She's growing bigger, Adam. It's like she was resized. Maybe we should bring in a doctor."

I attempt to discuss this with Kela, but she submerges herself underwater and refuses to come up. She speaks less and does not even comment when the news broadcasts a threat of Level-Six.

~

Kela's gone.

I search the house, briefly consider calling the police, and rummage my brain for her possible whereabouts.

Then I see my bag on my office chair. Papers stick out of its front compartment.

I fish for my key card but do not expect to find it.

Paranoia makes the drive to the Aquarium seem longer. I placate the guard who saw Kela (unspeaking and haggard, almost like in a disturbed trance), saying that she lost something of importance in the tank during one of her performances. He wipes his forehead and shares his opinion about Kela's deteriorating health. "She looks sick. No offence, sir, but she really does."

I turn on the green spotlight. It casts dancing shadows on the water's surface, with each new flash painting an increasingly eerie image. I peer in but can't see Kela. Is she not inside?

I am about to turn when I see a pair of what appears like valves open. I hold my breath and look again. At the next flash of light, I see Kela looking at me from the depth of the tank. She is like her mother now – a sea giant hidden in the darkness. I strip off my shirt and pants and dive into the water, letting the faint light guide me to her.

She reclines on the rock formation at the bottom, her hand guiding my feet to her collarbone. Her scales pulsate with a steady beat. I hike to her cheek and kneel before her right eye.

The air escapes my lungs. The last thing I remember is the white mound of her eye and its dilating pupil focusing on me.

~

K ela whispers my name.

"Adam. Adam, come back."

I wake up in bed, slightly dazed by the stream of light seeping through the blinds. Kela stares at me as though unsure if I am truly present. She touches my face with her scaly fingers. Blood oozes from the slash on my cheek from when she makes contact. She withdraws and apologizes.

"I dreamt of you," I tell her.

She nods. "I dreamt the same thing."

"Is that the future?"

"I believe it is."

She rotates her wedding ring until it's off her finger and then places it on my chest. This is the first time I had seen her let go of a shiny object.

SO YOU WANT ANOTHER REVOLUTION?

GABRIELA LEE

Ana saw the moon from her open kitchen window, where the heavy white orb hung low and unobscured in the sky. A faint aura of light surrounded it. Ana wondered if the moon knew about her, if it glanced her way through the window of her two-bedroom apartment on the seventeenth floor of a high-rise condominium and wondered about what she was doing. She questioned if the moon saw everything across the city: the shimmering electric lights around open windows and alleyways, the slow trickle of traffic moving up and down the streets and the glowing fields of chameleon fences that obstructed the rising concrete buildings which seemed to fill up the entire city.

The fences were designed to adapt to the peripheral vision of passers-by, creating shifting landscapes for pedestrians and drivers to hide the ugly skeletons of the buildings being built. She wondered how people lived beyond the artificial lights and landscape of her neighbourhood and wondered if they saw the same thing she did. She imagined taking a step onto the pavement beyond the lobby of the condo. Maybe she would see fields of flowers or swift-moving rivers, schools of deep-water fish swimming in HD technicolour, similar to the ones on her streaming screens whenever she had them on sleep mode.

Just the thought of her heel touching the dirty, germ-encrusted public sidewalks was enough. The outside world reminded her too much of her father. She remembered him not in the way that he was depicted in the old archives — his fist raised in painful anger, as he struggled to make his voice heard. She remembered him dancing in their garden when he heard the news of the old government falling and of freedom for the people. The Beatles were playing on the turntable in their living room and the music carried through the peaceful afternoon air. She remembered the golden light of summer, the abundant gumamela vines that grew in profusion across their walls—gray concrete static and dark, unlike the chameleon walls that changed with every passerby. *We all want to change the world*, the band sang, and Ana remembered dancing with her father as the walls of their world fell.

In the end, she thought her father placed too much faith in the people. - that they would do the right thing and care as much as he did. When they came for him, with their dirty fingers and dirtier words, Ana knew the world was contaminated and she didn't want anything to do with it.

What she didn't expect was that whatever stained her father affected her too.

So she hid and changed her face and her voice and her address. She lost touch with her mother and her family and anyone who ever mattered to her. She moved from city to city, province to province, making sure to leave no tracks in her wake. Even the name that she used here, now, didn't tether her to the past.

But despite everything, the voices could still find her.

They began creeping into the quiet of her mind once more, sinuously crawling through the open window and sliding across the kitchen floor. They wound their way around her limbs, slipping into her mind, oil-slick with sadness and misery. Anna hated the voices. They pleaded, prayed, and looked for answers in the silences between breaths. She wanted to escape the voices. Drowning in silence, she didn't notice the doorbell ringing until the third cycle.

She pulled herself away from the kitchen table and walked to the door, the money envelope that contained her grocery payment in her hand. She peered through the eyehole, taking note of the familiar yellow shirt and cap of the delivery man. He had a thin, angular face, and a smattering of facial hair across his chin. Ana wanted to think of him as generic — she had met a *lot* of delivery people ever since she moved into her unit — but there was something about the mischief in his eyes and a small smirk that played around the corners of his lips that made her think otherwise. She watched as he lifted a fist to the door and knocked sharply. "*Tao po*! SwiftFoot delivery for Ms. Ana Gitago!"

Ana opened the door, leaving a wide enough gap for the delivery man to slide her bag of groceries through. "Thank you," she whispered, holding out the payment with one hand and making sure that her skin didn't touch his. Who knew where his hand had gone the entire day?

The man stared at the envelope being held out to him. "How did you know the exact amount?"

"I get the same groceries every week."

"That sounds boring."

"It doesn't sound boring to me."

Ana was beginning to wonder if the man would ever get the money she was handing out. Her arm was starting to ache. He must have noticed the impatient expression on her face and finally passed the handle of the grocery bag. She tried to avoid his fingers but found herself brushing knuckles with the man. His hand felt uncomfortably warm. Hers would need a thorough disinfecting later.

He took the money and slipped it into his company-issued fanny pack. "Have a good evening," he said, nodding in her direction before stepping back to the elevator lobby. She watched his lanky form disappear down the hallway before closing the door, hoping that he wouldn't be the one to deliver her groceries the next time.

E nteng walked as casually as possible, knowing that the Client would be watching him. According to his brief, the Client was overly observant. The slight *click* that signified a door closing behind him only served to underscore that feeling of being watched.

As soon as he entered the elevator and the doors closed in front of him, he began unbuttoning his delivery shirt. The security camera at the corner whirled in his direction, the red light in the middle contracting and expanding as it focused on him.

Your report, Mr. Tolentino.

"She seems okay. Her window was open, and she seemed distracted. But she didn't try to get out," said Enteng, as he finished removing the shirt.

We'll send Maintenance over to deal with that.

"Okay," said Enteng.

Did she recognize you?

"Didn't seem like it."

Good.

He stood in his undershirt just as the elevator arrived at the ground floor and opened into a faux-marble lobby decorated with pots of snake plants, spider plants, and umbrella trees, as well as oil paintings of abstract shapes. Curved Scandinavian sofas filled most of the open space, and a crystal chandelier dripped from the ceiling. There were no other residents in the area. In fact, there were no other residents occupying the building—the government bought them out and relo-cated them when they learned where Ana Gitago... no, *Buencamino*, was.

Enteng walked towards the concierge, where a man in a crisp white *barong* nodded to him in acknowledgement. He nodded back, then slid behind the man, and entered a door marked *Administrative Office*.

The office was small and harshly lit, with a row of lockers lining one side of the room, and a set of office desks pushed against the opposite wall. On top of the desks were holo-screens monitoring the surveillance footage of the cameras set around the perimeter of the building, silently watching the ebb and flow of pedestrian traffic. Enteng walked towards his locker and fiddled with the combination lock. While most of the security in the entire building was state-of-the-art digital panels and wall inserts, the staff's security was minimal at best. A well-timed yank could have easily broken the lock that kept his locker door shut. He swapped his delivery uniform for an unremarkable polo shirt and slightly scruffy jeans, stuffing the yellow pants and button-down inside the locker, where they would remain until the next shift. Once he was done changing his clothes, he swung his ratty blue backpack over one shoulder and slammed the locker shut.

Dong, the shift monitor, arrived just as Enteng was leaving the room. "Don't forget, ha, you need to time out," the older man said.

Enteng waved the flimsy cardboard of his time card in front of Dong. "It was just the one time," he said as he sauntered over to the bundy clock mounted on the other end of the office, where another door was securely shut. "And it was raining. The time card got wet. Why don't they give us plastic ones?"

"Cost-cutting," answered Dong as he walked up to Enteng. He sounded slightly drunk, his voice slurring, unlike the voice he used on the loudspeaker in the elevator. "You know how it goes."

"She's the daughter of the last man who tried to overthrow the government, *and* she's the most powerful telepath in three generations. You would think that deserves better security, right?"

Dong shrugged. "I don't make the rules here."

Enteng slotted his time card through the slit across the top of the plastic bundy clock, hearing the slight screech-click of the machine as it printed the date and time. He slipped his card on the metal rack beside the clock and waved goodbye to Dong. "See you tomorrow, old man."

"Shut up, you idiot," groaned Dong as Enteng closed the door behind him.

As soon as he stepped out of the employees' exit, the building behind him shimmered, as if seen through an off-focus camera lens, before settling into the shape of a condominium tower under construction. Its tall metal spires jutted towards the sky with concrete pylons and slabs that would make up the bulk of the floors and glass panes with "X's" taped across them. A handful of backhoes and drills were parked at the side, and the ground, though still solid beneath Enteng's feet, took on the consistency and sheen of damp soil. Nobody would ever expect an actual building to be built entirely of chameleon walls, but this one was an experiment, funded by certain government departments. Enteng wasn't even quite sure who or what was involved in keeping the entire monstrosity operating, but he wasn't complaining. He needed a job and they were paying.

He walked towards the cement sidewalk, his feet sinking into the illusory soil. The chameleon walls that were used for Poppy Towers were of a different quality than the ones commonly used to cover construction sites and the images were a little too crisp, a little too real for Enteng's taste. He wanted to see pixels when the walls were trying to adjust to too many people, or the usual faded hues the images took on whenever only a handful of people were looking at them. He joined the throng of people jostling down the sidewalk, umbrellas blooming like dark flowers around him. He kept his head bare, his hands in his pockets, the smell of petrichor and cooling sweat surrounding him as he followed the crowd towards the nearest underground station.

Home was two hours away, just beyond the boundaries of Makati Phase 3, where many new residential developments were rising in the wake of the Last Uprising. Enteng lived in one of the two-storey ramshackle box housing that used to be part of housing sprawls, before the boundaries came down and the resources dried up. His family only had a working artesian well and a gasoline generator that sputtered and screamed whenever it ran for more than four hours, but he wasn't complaining. Some of his neighbours had it worse.

He raised his right hand, waiting for the security cams to identify him as a resident. There was a pause as the wall shimmered and allowed him passage. This was the entrance to Sapang Tubo which, from the main highway, looked like waving fields of grass with a mountain range in the horizon. Behind the wall, doors to homes were lit by naked incandescent bulbs or candles burning low, and narrow walkways branched off in different directions into the darkness. Puddles of water trickled down the walls, leaving the bare concrete perpetually damp and mould-encrusted. Several people who were still sitting on their front stoops nodded as he passed by and an old man muttered angrily behind his back. Enteng ignored him. He had been walking down the same road for the past ten years, since his parents passed away. He and Sofia moved into their house along with Jeph, their four-year-old son, his younger sister Mimi with her girlfriend Jack, and his cousin Anton, who was sometimes there, and sometimes not.

The lights were turned off when he arrived at the narrow gate and squeezed through. Plants grew in abundance in their front yard, the small concrete space filled with pots. Sofia loved trees, and although the tall ones were only found in small protected spaces, she easily cultivated smaller varieties at home and sold them to decorators in the city. The door was almost too low for him; he had to duck. Inside the house, people sprawled on the bare concrete mat, sleeping on thin rattan mats that protected them from the cold floor. Enteng tip-toed between each person, unsure why they were invited but nevertheless allowed them a night's slumber. He would have to talk to Mimi about partying inside the house.

There was a stack of empty beer bottles inside the kitchen sink, and they overran the kitchen counter. Enteng grabbed a garbage bag from under the sink and began gathering up the empty bottles, worried that Jeph might accidentally break the glass and hurt himself. There was some moonlight that filtered past the layers of rooftop edges and electricity poles, and he tried to move as quietly as possible. Once the bottles were all safely put away, he wiped his hands on his pants and moved towards the bedroom he shared with his wife and child.

Sofia's candle was flickering softly as he entered the room, casting a warm orange glow through the small space. She was reading a novel, the blanket pooled around her legs. She looked up, smiling, as he shed his backpack and pants on the floor, and slid into bed beside her. Jeph slept on a child-sized mat at the foot of their bed. Enteng made a mental note to search for second-hand bed frames for his son; he was getting too big for the mat.

She set aside the book and wrapped her arms around him. She was small and brown and fragrant in his arms, and Enteng felt his heart stutter at the utter joy that Sofia brought to his life, and how she miraculously decided to stick with him all those years.

"I missed you," she breathed in the space between their lips. He smiled and leaned towards her, breathing her in. The candle on the bedside table cast long shadows against the wall, capturing the dance of their lovemaking.

∾

He delivered Ana's groceries every week after that. They tried to make sure that everyone had a role in the ever-revolving cast of delivery people that brought her food and water, fixed her equipment, and de-clogged her drains, and even Dong made a memorable cameo as a cantankerous old locksmith who was brought in to help Ana unlock her bathroom door.

Enteng always tried to give her a kind word or tell her about the world outside. Sometimes, it would be little things; like how they swapped chicken for pork because prices were skyrocketing again, or news about the latest skirmishes between remnants of the Last Revolution's strike teams against state-sponsored bounty hunters, or the latest art installations across chameleon walls that were being used permanently in public parks and the walls of commercial buildings.

Ana would usually acknowledge his chatter with a nod and a smile, handing him the money in the envelope and waiting for him to leave.

But sometimes, she would pause and listen to him. Enteng didn't really mention these details in his reports. And once, he asked her why she never left her apartment. *Agoraphobia*, she whispered, before closing the door. He had to perform a quick online search. That was when he began telling her small stories, figuring that it wouldn't hurt her to know a little bit more about the world she was so afraid of entering.

~

J ust before he had to leave for his shift each morning, Enteng fired up the generator to charge everyone's electronics and clean the house. The old flatscreen was mounted on the wall in the living room. The mid-morning news was on while Enteng was vacuuming the floor. That was when Anton strolled into the small house. He smelled of the previous night's cigarettes and cheap alcohol, and an ecstatic look on his face. As the President's face flashed on the screen, his digitally augmented face appearing smooth and blemish-free, Anton threw up his middle finger at the screen. "Fucker," he said, the word easily rolling off his tongue.

"Watch it," Enteng said mildly.

"Oh right, you work for the Man," said Anton as he wandered to the fridge for a pitcher of cold water, and grabbed a glass from the dish rack on the kitchen counter.

"North Point is a private security enterprise," said Enteng.

On the screen, more new high-rise buildings were being created in the empty spaces of the old city, with bulldozers razing the old remnants of Metro Manila and smoothing over the soil for new construction projects. Shots of the manicured landscapes of the Makati Phases were interspersed with the smoking ruins of the city right after the Last Revolution, when over two-thirds of the country was razed and sold for scrap—both organic and inorganic—to other players in the theatre of war. Enteng was born a decade after the Last Revolution, but his parents had always told him that it was that damn telepath's fault. Hector Buencamino brainwashed the entire population into overthrowing the government and although his coup succeeded, the President's family brought in militant factions from other countries in order to control Buencamino's ragtag forces. In the end, Buencamino released his hold on the minds of the people under his control and submitted himself to the tender mercies of the government. He disappeared soon after.

"All security forces, private or otherwise, are under the military," said Anton. "You could be called or conscripted to fight in a war that you don't believe in, like our parents."

"I don't want to have this argument again, 'Ton."

"So what do you want to talk about? The Buencamino girl you're guarding in the fake condo tower?"

Enteng whipped around, the nozzle of the vacuum dropping from his hands. "How the fuck did you know that?"

Anton grinned wolfishly. "We have our share of inside sources."

"We?"

"Another revolution is brewing underneath the streets, Kuya Enteng. You've been pretending for far too long, hiding behind those stupid chameleon walls. You think those walls are just there for beautification? Let me tell you—that building is not the only one of its kind that this government is hiding." Anton slammed his water glass against the kitchen counter. "Anyone who could ever be called a threat to this government has been put away behind those screens and hidden away from view. You think prisons and torture chambers are gone just because we signed some treaty?"

"That sounds like a lot of paranoid ramblings," said Enteng. "You'd better watch what you say outside."

"But you don't deny that you're guarding the Buencamino girl?"

Enteng paused. "You know I can't say anything about that." He said down on one of the three chairs that circled the makeshift dining table that they had saved from one of the older ruins a few years ago.

Anton's face relaxed. "Sorry for yelling as well. I just came back from... well, here's the thing. We need your help."

"By yelling at me?" The news scroll had moved on to speculation on the prices of the newest real estate buildings, of the luxury builders that were advertising their latest developments, and how chameleon walls could be used in various ways, from landscaping to security to entertainment. But Enteng muted the volume and turned to his cousin. "Look, 'Ton, when we took you in, we promised we'd keep you out of trouble. But coming home late? Secret meetings? It's okay if you want to have bad feelings about the government, but maybe you should be more careful about who you talk to. Especially with my job on the line."

Anton waved his hand nonchalantly. "I promise you, this isn't going to get you fired or in trouble or anything. We just need you to pass something to Buencamino."

"From whom?"

"Her father."

Enteng felt something heavy and leaden fall in the pit of his stomach. It had been over thirty years. Hector Buencamino's name was all but forgotten. Certainly, the government had done its own work in burying his history; Enteng couldn't remember anything but scraps of information, and he wasn't even sure where he got them from.

"Kuya, do you really think that things are going well? Open your eyes. They're bleeding us for every centavo they can get. We're slowly marching to our own deaths." Anton slid a small metal cylinder across the table. It was a data tube, the kind you could insert in holo-screens or in digital home boxes to play music or flash images on a digital surface. It was as small as the tip of Enteng's pinky. "This is the message."

"What's inside?"

"A song. Just one file. You can even play it, if you want. It's public domain, so they can't even accuse us of piracy." Although no longer a criminal offence, most people still used piracy as an excuse to get back at those with whom they held a grudge against. "You can place it in your grocery delivery or whichever role you'll be playing today, so she'll find it."

"But what about me? They can easily trace it back to me. They've got cameras everywhere."

"We'll help you out there. Like I said, we've got a friend on the inside."

Enteng stared at the data tube. It seemed so small and innocuous. And it just contained a song, Anton said. Probably a keepsake from the old man, or to tell his daughter that he was still alive. Maybe to even give her hope. Enteng understood hope, he hoped to give his wife and child a better life outside the slums of Sapang Tubo. He hoped to be a better brother to Mimi, and to help Anton be a better person. He hoped that he could live out his older years in peace. But he also hoped that *everyone* could do that, not just him.

Perhaps Anton was right. Even though it was just a small step, he could still step up.

~

"Do you know what this is?" said Ana as she pulled out the data tube from the grocery bags Enteng had just delivered, staring at him sadly.

"My cousin says... it's from your father. That your father is alive."

For the first time since he had known her, she opened her door wider and ushered him inside. Once the door closed behind him, walked towards a nearby chair and sat in front of Enteng, facing him. "Of course I know my father is alive. I'm a telepath. You think I can't sense all of you?"

Enteng shook his head, flabbergasted. This was not how he had imagined this to go. "But you... you never leave the apartment."

"I *chose* to stay here. I asked to be placed in custody. When I bought this place, the President had me under house arrest as soon as I walked through the door. But we struck a deal. I stay here, I don't interfere with his... plans, and in return, my father is kept alive. Of course, I don't know where he is. They keep on moving him randomly, so it's difficult to track him down, and even he doesn't know where he's headed most of the time. Did you know that you can't read the minds of everyone?"

"So you know all about us?"

Ana gestured to a small crystal bowl on the kitchen counter, beside knick-knacks and other kitchen ornaments. It was filled to the brim with similar data tubes. "You're not the first one who tried to smuggle a Beatles song in here."

"So why are you still doing this?"

Ana shrugged. "It keeps my father's friends happy to keep on discovering where I am. It keeps my father happy to know that they're still trying to look for him. And whichever way the wind blows, I know that I'll still be kept here, and I'll be comfortable." She sat down on the table. "You have to understand that I don't want to leave this place. I don't want to go down the elevator and out into the streets. I am fine watching the world go by. I can get everything I need with a push of a button."

Enteng hung his head, trying not to show her his embarrassment. For one, shining moment, he had hoped that his actions would lead to something, anything. But it was all shattered right here, by the person that Anton had placed his hopes in. For at least an instant, Enteng had felt the same way.

"Now that you know about my little secret, you have to understand that I also have ways of making sure that you can't talk about it, right?" Ana said. Her eyes were calm as she said this. "I've already read all about your little family in Sapang Tubo, and it would really be a shame if they suddenly disappeared one night, am I correct?"

"You wouldn't."

"If it keeps my father safe, and keeps me comfortable, you'd be surprised at what I'm capable of doing."

"So I keep my head down and shut up, and you'll stay here, and everything stays the way they are?"

Ana nodded. "Yes. Well, except for one thing..."

The music in the elevator was the same old song, some Beatles tune that he couldn't quite identify. But Enteng had a job to do, and it wasn't to critique the music. He couldn't quite believe that he was so lucky to have gotten the job with North Point Security. They were one of the toughest employers, and he was just pleased that he was able to rise through the ranks to get here–the prime spot at Poppy Towers, where the most powerful telepath in the world, Ana Buencamino, lived.

Of course, she didn't go by that name. The name on the lease was Ana Gitago. But Enteng knew that everything was a sham with the building, the condo, even the chameleon walls surrounding the site, hiding everything in plain sight. They were simply making sure that she was well-taken care of.

Today was the first day that he would meet her.

He made sure that the grocery delivery logo patch was clearly displayed on his chest, and that the two grocery bags he carried in one hand were still sturdy. Nothing had broken, nothing had fallen out. He had never been part of the security team that checked on her before, and he was thankful that Dong, his boss, had given him the opportunity. He could hear the slight mechanized shift of the cameras embedded on the ceilings as they followed him out of the elevator.

1331. That was her unit number. He raised his hand and knocked sharply. "*Tao po*! SwiftFoot delivery for Ms. Ana Gitago!"

It took a few seconds before he heard the latch sliding from its cradle, and the door swinging slightly open. She peered from behind the door, her long, straight hair covering most of her features like rainwater. He could see moonlight streaming from the open window behind her. He should tell his boss about that. He lifted the groceries from his hand so that she could take them. He could see her cringe as her fingers brushed his accidentally.

"Thank you," she whispered, as she placed the groceries on a nearby countertop. Returning to the door, she held out the payment with her other hand, making sure that her skin didn't touch his.

He stared at her for a long time. "You look like someone I know," he said

She shook her head. "Take the money."

But Enteng couldn't seem to make his limbs move. There was something familiar about the moment: as though he had been here before, but couldn't seem to make sense of it. His memory stuttered, stuck on repeat. He couldn't even remember what this was called – it was some sort of French term, surely Sofia would know…

"*Déjà vu*," said the woman in front of her. She peered at him with a single eye from beneath the long ropes of her hair. "But don't worry. It will pass."

Enteng reached out and took the money from her hands, almost as though his limbs had taken on a life of their own. "Wait," he said. "How did you – "

But he was never able to finish his sentence. She had already closed the door in front of him.

ON THE ROAD TO BIRINGAN

JOSEPH F. NACINO

The old Japanese man came to the city of Biringan on the island of Samar a little before dusk, just as the sun had settled past the horizon.

His skin darkened from years under the sun, the old man was dressed as a common Filipino farmer. A plain shirt, trousers, and a wide-brimmed straw hat covering the thatch of white hair on his head. On his feet were a pair of wooden clogs he had made himself. On his back, he carried a stack of firewood tied with a cord. This stack hid a ubiquitous wooden stick made of narra, more than three feet in length, fire-hardened and carefully polished to a deep brown colour.

Despite the weight of the bundle of wood, the old man carried himself straight with a warrior's bearing, and his gaze was still sharp as he took in the surrounding forest. His grip on the cord that held the wooden bundle on his back was firm and steady.

He had heard so many things about Biringan and its other names, such as the Black City and the Invisible City. Some called it the *Place to Find the Lost*, and he hoped the last would prove true for him.

He had followed the advice of a wise woman, a *babaylan* who had hidden herself from the Spanish monks intent on destroying the old faith of the land, in finding the path that led to the city. For a time, it had felt as if someone else had taken control of his body as he walked through the undergrowth. But as the sun set, he felt like himself again.

He was still in the forest, but the trees seemed older and primeval. The ancient trees stood verdant and majestic around him, clothed in layers of moss like royal cloaks. They reminded him of the Aokigahara, the Sea of Forests that surrounded Mount Fuji. When he was growing up, he had heard that forest had also served as a doorway to the underworld and the home of the *yūrei*, or the spirits of the dead.

"It's good to be back again," said Simeon, the spirit in the wooden stick. For a moment, there was a faint smell of tobacco and a glimmer of red eyes peeking from the bundle on his back.

The old man looked around and said in a soft, measured tone: "I see no difference here."

"You humans are blind to many things," Simeon muttered.

"Is there any difference for you when you see the Spanish, Filipinos and us Japanese?" the old man asked.

"You humans are all the same to us. White, brown, yellow skin… Always taking things that don't belong to you."

"Humans, monsters… we are all blind somehow. What matters is how we open our eyes to see what we normally do not see," he shot back.

"Another saying from your homeland?" Simeon said in a mocking tone.

"A more universal way of thinking," he replied. "Where do we go from here?"

"Follow the light of the sunset. There, you will find the city… and maybe, this angel that you seek," the spirit directed and lapsed back into sulking silence.

∽

In a previous life, the old man's name was Takayama Ukon, or Justo, and he had been a warrior like his father before him, a samurai and daimyo.

Following his father, Ukon remained a *kirishitan* even as he and his family had lost their holdings and their status in the wake of growing anti-Christian sentiment. When Tokugawa Ieyasu finally ordered all Christians to be expelled from Japan, Ukon led others Japanese Christians, as well as his own family, to the capital of the Philippines.

In Manila, they were warmly welcomed by the Spanish Jesuits and their subjects. The refugees were housed in the small suburb of Dilao, where many of the other Japanese migrants lived. Ukon himself was received by the Governor General, who slyly hinted of Spanish support for a possible uprising of Christian Japanese back home. However, Ukon refused to be part of the world again. He was an old man already, and he had lived a full life, one full of both turbulence and gentleness. Ukon had no illusions about the time left, with a wife and four children dead, two at infancy. His daughter and remaining son had families of their own, his lord and country disowned him, and his sword was broken. All he had left was his faith and his belief in God. He felt he was ready to die.

However, several days after arriving, he found his attitude changing. Seated on a stone bench in a small garden festooned with the amaryllis flowers, he had stretched out his hand to watch dust motes dance in the light. That's when he heard a female voice ask him in perfect Japanese, "What do you see?"

"I see that the light this far from my home is still the same."

A young Filipino woman stood behind him, carrying a basket of laundry. For a moment, he thought an angel stood before him—though it was not her beauty that stunned him.

With a round-shaped face with plump cheeks, the young woman had a slightly golden hue to her brown skin. Ukon felt her piercing dark eyes astutely cut through the hidden deceptions and comforting lies that banded his soul together. Her glow resembled the halo that surrounded the Virgin Mary in the oil paintings displayed at churches.

"How is it that you speak my language so well?" he asked.

The young woman placed the basket beside him on the bench. She untied the scarf on her head to reveal long dark hair and used the cloth to wipe perspiration from her forehead.

"I've lived with your people for many years now," she said. "I've even come to learn about your history and culture."

Ukon nodded and looked away. "I am at a disadvantage then. I hardly know anything about your language and your country."

"It's always good to be open about new things. I come from a place far from Manila, and I'm also learning new things as well," she replied with a smile.

"Well then, I hope you can teach me. Not too late for someone as old as myself to learn something new."

"Good. My name is Isabel. What is yours?"

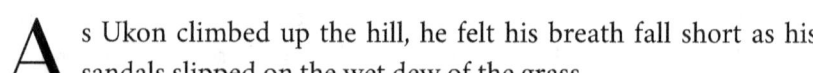

A s Ukon climbed up the hill, he felt his breath fall short as his sandals slipped on the wet dew of the grass.

He missed the days of his youth. He remembered running up hills of similar height in full battle armour, an army behind him with their banners unfurled, and his father at his side. Back then, he was full of fear but he kept it at bay, more afraid of shaming his father. He still had the code that had guided him for most of his life.

"We're almost there," said Simeon.

"How can you tell?"

"Do you see the light?"

That was when he noticed the soft blue glow that emanated from the top of the hill, more noticeable now that evening had fallen.

He presumed that evening had fallen as he had lost all sense of time. The sky had darkened but the grey clouds obscured the moon and the stars. Fortunately, there was a certain lightness in the darkness that made it possible for him to the path he was walking on. He couldn't discern how this was possible, as there was no source of light anywhere. It was also cooler here, unlike the rest of the country.

Wherever this Biringan was, it was certainly different from most of the areas of the Philippines. On his journey, he had spent many days travelling through small dusty roads patrolled by Spanish troops. He sometimes rested under the bushes during the hot and humid after-noons, when the roads gave no shelter from the summer sun and he had to fan himself with one of the giant leaves of a banana tree.

At night, he couldn't travel as much because it was too dark to see. That was when he made a fire and roasted whatever he had caught during the day. If he was unlucky, he would eat the salted fish he had stored away in his pack.

Based on what he'd learned from Isabel, her country had no castles, just a smattering of towns and communities scattered throughout the archipelago. There was the walled city of Manila, of course, as well as Cebu and the other settlements where the Spanish and the Catholic Church had left their mark. In rural areas, they required the natives to build small churches through forced labour or *polo*.

"Stop thinking that, this is still the land where you came from!" barked the spirit.

"Can you read my mind now?"

"No, but you humans are predictable. I know what you're thinking. You're thinking that you are still in human lands," Simeon replied. "If you keep doing that, you will make a terrible mistake—and *snap!* I will be free, and eat you up!"

Ukon was still not used to having a demon on hand, bound as it was in a bundle of wood, much more having a conversation with one. One time, he and Isabel discussed the myths of their lands, something Isabel was quite well-versed in. It was then she told him the different ways of defeating the monsters. He had told Isabel that in his country, there were *yōkai* similar to *oni* - giant ogre-like beings with ferocious faces, sharp claws, and wild hair.

This country also had their share of giants, it seemed, though Isabel had called Simeon with his tall height, ebony skin, red eyes, and sharp teeth a *kapre*. This monster reminded Ukon of his childhood stories of the yokai giant, the *Daidarabotchi*. It was Isabel who had taught Ukon how to bind one to a piece of wood, lured with a smoking piece of tobacco that they found irresistible.

It was strange the things he remembered from the many conversations he had with her. Fortunately, this one seemed to have proven useful.

Ukon finally crested the summit of the hill and saw the source of the blue light.

Before him lay Biringan, and he saw why this sprawling place surrounded by ancient trees would never have been mistaken for a human city. For one, the towers that loomed over the city were higher than the forest, covered with shrubbery and ivy. Some sections and ledges even had sturdy trees on them. Beneath was what seemed to be black marble, but it looked too fluid to be stone. This made the city appear to be raised from one piece, its buildings—as large as cathedrals—rising high and connected to each other with too-thin bridges that gave a liquid-like appearance to its facade.

The buildings were also festooned with faint blue flickering lights, and Ukon realized that the flickering was due to their fluttering of a thousand wings. Meanwhile, the full moon cast a pale light on the whole cityscape made even softer by the mist that threaded its way around the buildings.

He felt tears fall from his eyes. "Time to see and learn new things again."

W hen Isabel told him what she really was, he had a time believing it. More importantly, his faith—and what he had been taught by the Roman Catholic Church—made him disbelieve it.

At the time, he had been gently inquiring on Isabel's beliefs. He knew she hadn't converted to Christianity yet. That was when she laughed and told him she was a demon.

"Don't tease me. You aren't a demon," he said, almost reaching out to touch her arm. The two of them were walking through the cobble-stone streets of Intramuros that morning. "You're human, but you're never too evil to be redeemed by our Savior."

She laughed again, a throaty outburst that was so different from the prim Spanish young women hiding their faces behind hand fans and gliding past them. She said: "Dom Justo, I am real as you, or the banana seller there. But the *Banwaanon* are not regarded as humans, as you Christians see us. And it's true. Well, at least most of us look human. But still, you call us demons and regard us as evil."

As she explained it to him, many of the *Banwaanon*—or the People of the Forest—lived on the different islands of the archipelago. But most of them lived in Biringan.

It was there, she said, that she had been born and raised by her human father who had been brought there by her mother who was an *engkanto*, or spirit of the forest.

"In my land, the *yōkai* were dangerous demons that lured my coun-trymen into the darkness of the woods and ate them."

"But were they really demons—or was that something that was taught to you by those afraid of what they didn't know?"

Ukon glanced at her. The old man found it unsettling that he was talking of legends beings as if they were humans instead of...demons, as the Church had proclaimed them to be.

"I've heard the accusations against my people so many times. We are the same as all Filipinos living under the thumb of the Spanish conquerors. But my people have been forced to hide in the mountains and valleys by the Church because we are being burned out of our forest homes. They call us demons and say we eat babies. But we only want to be left alone to live our lives in peace."

Ukon was troubled by that. In his homeland, his faith in God had made him a target by the government, like Isabel's people. However, this also meant that the Church was wrong about those they called evil spirits.

"That is... something I must think about," Ukon said.

Isabel smile in response seemed to brighten the world around him. She said: "It's all right. I need to go now to buy lunch for my Japanese *amo*. But let's meet again tomorrow to talk about this."

But the next day, Isabel did not appear, and the day after that. That was when Ukon found out that she had completely disappeared. Even her Japanese employer was mystified with Isabel's departure, for she had left all her personal belongings behind.

The leaves that crunched underneath Ukon's feet even echoed around him as they travelled along the path. Meanwhile, Simeon kept a constant commentary as he pointed out things in their surroundings. Ukon felt a sense of pride emanating from his companion.

"The old trees serve as the home of my people. They allow us to live peacefully inside them with halls that can be larger than the biggest church made by humans. Look up."

Ukon saw lights from giant shadowed houses cradled in the branches of trees, as well as small bridges made from vines connecting one tree to others.

"We like to visit each other so we usually travel around through those bridges. Also keeps our houses private from those travelling below, like humans."

"We don't see any of this in the human world?" Ukon asked, awed by the vast inter-connected roads that lay just above his head.

"No, everything is hidden. Each tree has doors located both here and in the human realm, since they're rooted in both worlds. That's why our people get mad when humans decide to clear forests for their farms without talking to us. I mean, how would you like it if someone decided to destroy your house while you're inside it?"

"Understandable," the old man said.

Soon, they saw people also walking on the path heading towards the city. Simeon said: "The large market that surrounds the gate of the city is always open. Constantly there are people heading to the city."

Most of the people on the road ignored Ukon as they walked. The old man was surprised to see the variety of travellers, including ones which resembled humans.

Most of them wore simple black clothing, from trousers to shirts. Although they appeared human, a quick glance at their faces showed they were missing the vertical groove between the base of the nose and the border of the upper lip. He thought that these were the *Banwaanon* that Isabel had told him.

For a moment Ukon was distracted by whistling coming from the bundle of wood he was carrying.

"Are you... happy?" he asked.

"What?" Simeon sounded defensive. "Is it wrong to whistle?"

Returning to his observations, Ukon saw that the others on the road ran the gamut from the strange to the grotesque. For example, there were beings with equine head and faces, human torsos with back legs of horses that made them stand taller than humans. There was a body wearing only a loincloth but had no head, as well as a group of naked dwarf-like beings with long, white beards that hid their private parts and *salakot* straw hats on top of their heads.

"What is that smell? Do you smell that?" Bright eyes flared in the bundle.

"Smell what?" he asked.

"I think... tobacco! From the far north! From Ilocos!" Simeon exclaimed. "Those are rare down here! Who's the lucky bastard who has that, I wonder..."

Ukon shook his head. Given that Simeon was mostly sarcastic in his statements, he wasn't used to the now-loquacious spirit.

He heard giggling behind him and turned to see a gigantic creature with a single eye in the middle of its forehead. It had huge upper lips and two long tusks that jutted from its mouth. It was incongruous to hear such a sound from a menacing being.

Flying above were half-human and half-avian creatures, faces dominated by huge beaks with long fingers, and feet that pointed backwards. He was about to ask Simeon what they were, but his companion appeared to be distracted again, whistling a jaunty tune.

Ukon saw a hairy, wild, man-sized ape with long nails swinging through the trees, and a couple of humanoid giants with big feet, their bodies covered in black hair, and deep rumbling voices as they conversed quietly to themselves.

He jumped when he saw a pale-faced lady dressed in all white floating down the road, reminding him of *yuki-onna*, the snow woman. She even left a cold feeling that ran up Ukon's spine.

The flapping of wings made him look upward. The upper half-torso of a woman with bat wings flew low overhead, her entrails dangling behind her.

"Don't stare," Simeon told him. "It's not polite. Staring is the same as looking up a woman's skirt." Ukon averted his stare.

There were a number of animals on the road, ranging from a pack of black hogs to a handful of lone black dogs. All of them had red eyes that glowed in the dark.

However, the dogs avoided a beast that growled at them when they came too near it. This beast had a cowlike body, large head, shaggy coat of hair, and a monstrous mouth with two pairs of huge tusklike incisors jutting out of it.

Simon whispered to him, "Hmmm. That *mantabungal* is far from home. They're a short-tempered, hungry lot, and they have a tendency to ravage everything in their path."

One of the black dogs glanced at him and scampered towards him. As the dog approached, it changed its appearance to a humanoid form, except for cat-like eyes and bat wings on its back.

"Dom Justo! I am glad to see you made it here!" proclaimed the creature. "I apologize I couldn't lead you to Biringan. I didn't know myself I would be coming here! My kind are currently celebrating a moveable feast! It's an epicure's ritual that only we *berbalang* hold on to, you know, and it takes us across many graveyards. If not for my prior obligations, I would have certainly helped to bring you here. But still, I am glad you made it and I laud you for your determination!"

Ukon recognized the loquacious creature as Elizalde, the one who had given him Isabel's last message and had also helped him get away from the city. He gave a slight nod of his head and responded. "Regardless, thank you again for your help, Elizalde."

As Elizalde gave a farewell wave and joined his companions again, Simeon said grudgingly: "I wouldn't have thought you would be friends with a *berbalang*. As cadaver-eaters, their mouths stink quite terribly. Even my tobacco smoke can't hide it."

"Yes, it took a while to get used to," Ukon admitted.

~

U kon would have gone to search for Isabel sooner, except that he was laid low by a fever for several days. The sickness was so terrible that many of his Japanese companions as well as the Spanish officials and priests that visited his room in the *bahay na bato* thought he would not survive.

But then his fever broke, and he woke up to the sound of rain falling against the sliding windows of wood and capiz shells. He had many vivid dreams while sick, but the ones that remained with him when he woke up revolved around Isabel calling to him and beseeching his help.

"Isabel?" he said in the darkness of the room.

"Not her," moaned a voice.

Ukon jumped backward on the wooden bed and wished he had his sword once more. "Who's there?"

A figure laughed and raised itself from the shadow beside the wooden *aparador* that held all his belongings. "Terribly sorry about that. I couldn't resist playing as a ghost. But I am more substantial than other spirits. I bring a message from a mutual friend of ours."

That was when Ukon caught the smell of rotting meat that reminded him of mutilated bodies under the sun for days and of battles that churned the ground red with blood.

"Who are you?" he asked, trying to calm his racing heart.

The figure came forward. The first thing Ukon noticed was the small bat-wings attached to its back. The second thing he noticed was that its eyes had a faint glow like fireflies. The creature's skin had the pallor of dead things, and its smile—while friendly—was full of sharp teeth.

It bowed before speaking. "My name is Elizalde. Isabel told me to introduce myself properly because you are not knowledgeable about what we are. I am a *berbalang*. I haunt graveyards and burial grounds for my daily repast."

Elizalde looked around curiously. "I must say because I've been meaning to say this for some time now, but I had no one to talk to while I sat in the dark. In any case, this is the first time myself to be in a human house and it's quite interesting, to say the least."

Ukon sat up on the side of his bed, still wary, and said, "I would welcome you to this house, but I myself am just a guest here."

Elizalde perked up. "Are we not all guests in this existence given to us by the god of all, *Bathala*? We *berbalang* prefer our meal freshly dead, something that you humans also prefer, if I heard right. Though I don't believe I will ever understand the concept of cooking one's meal. In any case, we try to be considerate, which is why we leave a log of wood with an illusion cast on it to resemble the dead person we consume from funerals. We firmly believe it's always good to be polite to each other."

A polite ghoul? Will wonders never cease?

"Going back to our original topic, what was Isabel's message?" he asked.

"Oh yes! She apologized for leaving abruptly and without giving her farewells, as a terrible event has forced her to go home. But she said if you are determined, to come and find her in the city of Biringan on the island of Samar. She believes that you can help us in some way."

"Samar? That is many miles from here, and across the water."

Elizalde nodded. "Unfortunately, I have other things to do so I cannot accompany you on this trip. But I can advise you to seek the help of the *babaylan* who lives on the shore of the Pasig River. She will tell you how to get past the walls that hide Biringan."

"Hide? What do you mean?"

"Ah, you do not know," it sighed. "Biringan is a city with many spirits that make this land their home, including the *Banwaanon*, even if many of them prefer to live in the forests. This is because Biringan serves as a place of conclave where they gather and speak on the issues that they face. It has been concealed from human eyes for many years as part of the agreement reached between us and the Spanish priests. You will need to enact certain rituals to breach what has been veiled. Heed my advice, seek the *babaylan*. She can help you."

"Wait!" Ukon protested. "I cannot just leave here. My people expect so much from me and the Spanish will not just let me be."

The creature thought for a while and then said cheerfully, "May this help you with your decision." It snapped its fingers and leap through the open sliding windows into the night.

The old man felt something behind him and turned to see a body lying in his bed. It looked like him, but was pale and lifeless. When Ukon touched the body, it changed into an ordinary banana trunk shorn of its leaves. When he let go, it reverted to its illusion.

"God, what have I gotten myself into?" he asked, half in wonder and half in prayer.

That very night, he borrowed clothes hanging from a nearby washing line that would allow him to go unnoticed in the country and walked away from the remainder of his life. Despite still feeling weak from the fever that had recently struck him, he felt motivated by a different energy: the feeling that he was *needed*.

It took him several months to walk from Manila to Samar, having to pay a fisherman to take him on his boat across the waters that separated the two large islands. It was a torturous affair given the small size of the man's *bangka* and the choppy waters that threatened to swamp it. The galleon that had brought him to the Philippines was a hundred times larger and sturdier than any of the *bangka* he'd seen.

Later, he heard that the Spanish government and the Church had honoured his corpse with a state burial. He shook his head in bemusement at the fact that a log now rested in his grave. He wondered how far his faith in God had brought him that he—a warrior from a different nation—would be held in such high regard by foreigners in a strange land.

During his travel, he picked up a bundle of wood to complete his disguise as a farmer from the countryside. From this bundle, he selected one that fit the length he needed to craft it into a familiar shape of a *bokken*, or a wooden practice sword they normally used at home.

This became quite useful one night when a malevolent spirit confronted him while he was walking with the moon as his only light. Fortunately, he remembered what Isabel told him. Afterward, the spirit, which he had managed to trap in the *bokken*, gave his name as Simeon.

The spirit sometimes gave rather helpful advice in dealing with the other spirits and provided insightful conversations on the lonely road to Biringan. Suffice it to say, it was a more interesting journey once he had a companion on the road.

As he arrived at the open gates of the city, he saw before him an army of monsters and spirits led by Isabel in full battle gear, mounted on a horse.

"You're here," she said with a beatific smile.

Ukon looked down in embarrassment. "I came because you asked."

"I'm glad," she responded. "My people seek your help. Time passes swiftly outside Biringan, and a new wave of invaders called the British have defeated the Spanish to take away our lands and our freedom. Our oracles said a warrior from a far-away nation would come to aid us and I had a secret hope that this warrior was you."

"I've turned away from the warrior's path. You know that," he said, almost reproachfully.

"You were a warrior for your God," she corrected. "You carried both a sword and cross for many years in your land before you gave up your sword for your faith."

Abashed, he shook his head. "I'm too old for this. I'm too old for matters of the heart and of warfare."

Isabel laughed, though he didn't feel that she was mocking him. "You can never be too old. "I've wandered this land for many more years than you've been alive, so I know what you mean. It feels like time should have already passed us by and burdened other, younger shoulders with our responsibilities. But we have been put on this earth to fulfil the roles we've been given, so who are we to turn away from it?"

With that, she extended her hand to him. When he reached out to take it, he saw that his own hand had become younger, with the liver spots that had once dotted his skin now gone.

As Isabel pulled him up on her horse, he let go of the wooden bundle on his back except for the *bokken* that held the spirit of the *kapre*. He felt Simeon growl.

"I see you made a friend on your journeys," Isabel said.

Ukon replied, "He grows on you."

"I'm not your friend!" Simeon snapped back.

Ukon looked at Isabel thoughtfully. "So, an oracle foretold my arrival? Did you know that I would have come? Or what my answer would have been?"

Isabel looked amused. "Hasn't your god taught you anything? Our paths may be laid out for us, but it's always our choices that matter in the end."

Ukon chuckled at that. "You do know that I won't give up my faith for you? And that I aim to convert everyone here in Biringan to the worship of my God?"

Isabel laughed. "You can try."

Together, they rode off at the front of the army on the road leading away from Biringan.

LUKSAW

J.A.W. MCCARTHY

Aggie wasn't thinking about what she wanted when the image appeared on her bedroom wall. It wasn't like in third grade—the first time she was really aware of what she could do—when everyone was gasping and giggling and pointing as an image of Mrs. Patterson with her hair on fire materialized on the wall just over the crabby old teacher's shoulder. It wasn't like the story her parents once told her—how they found her standing in her crib one morning when she was barely two, staring at the wall as wisps of smoke floated up from the lines on the plaster that developed into a photo-perfect image of her lost stuffed bunny before their eyes. This time, when the image of the girl appeared on her bedroom wall, Aggie was thinking about the symphony of cats yowling outside her window.

Leaning as far as she could outside the window, Aggie poured fresh kibble into the big casserole dish on the grass below, the plinking of the food against ceramic drawing the usual two strays from the bushes across the yard. In the time it took her to close the window and put the kibble bag back under her bed, the girl on her wall had come together, arms filling out a stiff white blouse, legs emerging from beneath a dark green plaid skirt, face surfacing on the pebbly white paint like cereal floating in milk. Aggie let the smoke from the image roll over her shoulders rather than open the window again.

The girl was familiar, though not a TV celebrity or an old friend. Dark eyes, skin deeper than her mother's even when she let the sun touch her, lips that were smudged with wiped-off lipstick. She looked like a Catholic school girl, seventh grade maybe—Aggie knew the forced, uneasy smile and uneven stance of that age—from a time when students carried their books tied with string. It was a picture a proud parent would take against a blank wall between the couch and the front door.

As with the other sporadic images that had appeared when she was alone, Aggie decided she wouldn't tell her mother. Being a pediatric nurse, her mother knew what happened to kids who could do unbelievable things, and she'd spent enough late nights and early mornings shakily scrubbing lost bunnies and chocolate cakes and armless grade school bullies from the walls. Instead, Aggie grabbed an old t-shirt from her hamper and pinned it up over the image on the wall. In the morning, before her mother got home, she would get the bucket and sponge.

~

When Aggie came downstairs the next morning she found her mother squinting at something in the tall bookcase by the front door.

"I must be really tired," Julia said, offering her daughter a nervous smile. She was still in her dark blue scrubs, as if she had been standing at the bookcase since she got home.

"What's wrong?" Aggie asked.

Julia pulled a framed photo from its position between the thesaurus and an ancient copy of *The Joy of Cooking* and blinked at it a couple of times before handing it over.

Aggie had spent the first two years after her father died staring at this photo on her way out the door every single day; her finger had even left a permanent oily smudge on the glass where she always touched his cheek to say goodbye. Their trip to Disneyland seven years ago had been their last together, carefully planned even when they had the money for such indulgences. Aggie found herself smiling even now to see her dad in Mickey Mouse ears, cheeks stretched in a goofy grin as he held her and her mother close. She used to look at her ten-year-old self with disdain on the bad days and indifference on the best, but this morning, with her mother anxiously looking on, she felt neither. She saw what her mother had been hoping was only a trick of the light and overworked eyes.

"That's not...I wasn't wearing that," Aggie said, shoving the photo back at her mother. The little girl in the picture had Aggie's brown hair and braces, but she was wearing the same green plaid uniform as the girl who had appeared on the wall last night.

"Yeah, I remember you wearing your mermaid t-shirt in this picture," Julia agreed. She slid the photo back into the bookcase and ran her knuckles roughly over her eyes. "I mean, it's possible my memory's fading, but you're far too young for that, kid."

"Why would I be wearing a school uniform at Disneyland? I didn't go to Catholic school. I don't even know anyone who went to Catholic school."

"Your grandmother did," Julia shrugged.

Aggie wanted to turn the photo around because her father's smile seemed like a betrayal now, the cruel joke of a memory that was suddenly wrong and tainted by someone who wanted to hurt her. Perhaps the same someone she had just scrubbed from her bedroom wall.

"What the fuck, Mom?"

Her mother stopped to kiss the top of her head on her way to the stairs. "I shouldn't have said anything, Aggs. I'm tired, it's an old photo...I don't know why I noticed it. The photo paper's probably deteriorating, oxidizing—that's why it's green. There's oatmeal in the fridge. Go heat it up and get yourself to school."

~

V an separated sections of Aggie's long dark hair, taking the time to wrap each tendril around his fingers, then releasing them into soft waves against her bare shoulder. Aggie liked his big hands and all of the places they had been, how they never hesitated at all of the places she wanted them to go.

"Seriously? You're doing that again?" he teased her as she leaned across him to turn the framed photo on her nightstand face-down. "Even if it feels like you're being watched, it's us, Aggs. We're watching ourselves. Some people think that's hot."

"Yeah, but it's us at your sister's wedding. In a church. With Jesus on the cross in the background."

"I hate to break it to you, babe, but it doesn't matter if you turn the picture over—he's always watching, if you believe in that stuff."

Aggie felt Van's hands on her ass as she tried to slide back into her spot on the bed. He pretended to spank her, but his hand paused on her right cheek, fingers drawing a soft line across her skin.

"What's this?"

"Um, you've seen it before, dummy."

"No, I mean *this*. These marks." He held her across his lap as she tried to pull away. "Are those scars?"

Aggie got out of bed and went to her vanity, standing on her tiptoes as she pulled up the back of her t-shirt so she could see what her boyfriend was talking about. There, reflected back at her in the mirror, was a meshwork of puffy pink lines crisscrossing both of her ass cheeks. After a held-breath moment she touched one of the marks, but it didn't hurt. Each ugly line she traced was as benign and familiar as a long-healed scar.

"Are you okay? What happened to you?"

In the mirror, behind her still-frozen reflection, Aggie could see Van's legs swinging out from beneath the pale blue sheets. She dove for her underwear on the floor and quickly pulled them on. "I'm fine," she said briskly as he came up behind her. When his hand started to move down her back, she swatted him away. "It's probably just an allergic reaction. Maybe I'm allergic to you."

~

Aggie's grandmother used to say that she was dropped fully-formed into the jungle, sheltered by the bamboo and raised by the gibbons and the leopard cats and even the cobras that made a wide arc around her footsteps. In her mind, she had grown up as wild as the wolves that raised the unmannered in the country where she finally settled.

"No mother, no father," Grandmother would say with a wistful little laugh.

"What about the nuns who raised you?" Aggie once asked.

Grandmother just shook her head and said, "They don't count. They weren't even human."

"Were they mean to you because you could do what I can do?" Aggie asked, picturing herself on Space Mountain in elaborate detail, though the wall in front of them remained blank despite her efforts.

"No, I couldn't do what you can, my little Agnes," Grandmother said. "If everyone could see what I wanted...it would've been bad. It would have been much worse for me."

Often, when Aggie's grandmother started talking about the orphanage and the nuns and all the times she had climbed out the dormitory's second storey windows, Aggie's mother would say, "C'mon, Mommy, stop it, you're scaring her" and send little Aggie outside to play. Stories about the cobras and the jungle were met with an exasperated laugh and an epilogue of "Grandma sure has some imagination, doesn't she?", but anything about the place where Grandmother was really raised made Julia's whole body tighten up. Aggie only got to hear those stories—the ones that kept her awake and made her glad she was a little girl now and not then—on the nights when she and her grandmother were alone, waiting for her mother and father to get back from a dinner party or a movie.

The stories about escape attempts and pilfered whisky and forgetting to answer in English often ended in beatings with a metal-edged ruler, just like all stories about cruel nuns often do, except Grandmother had to pull down her underwear in front of everyone. Aggie thought about this now as she stared at her pink-ribboned ass cheeks again in the mirror; even hours later, after a hot shower and clean clothes, the marks were still there, a tangled puffy highway butting against her fingertips.

She had never been in an orphanage. She had never met a nun. Her parents had never laid a hand on her, not even when she pulled a knife from the counter or rolled the car into the street. She would look for burrs in her pants or evidence of bugs in her sheets, but she knew better. This was like the now-ghostly impression of the girl on her wall, appearing out of nowhere and lingering even after being scrubbed clean.

As Aggie was getting into bed, the cats started up again. After she poured the kibble, she stayed at the window and watched as a third, larger cat joined the usual two. He looked a bit rough with a chewed ear and stunted whiskers on one side of his face, but he wasn't particularly aggressive as he made a place for himself among the others. When the food was mostly gone, the two smaller cats remained to pick at the crumbs. Although one was bigger, their stripes matched, making them seem like mother and child. Their heads bobbed in unison, their tails curling and uncurling in opposite directions, a slow conduction, perfectly in sync.

∾

When Aggie was little, before she understood how dangerous it was, she tried to prove to her friends what she could do. The fact that none of her classmates believed that she was responsible for the image of their third-grade teacher with her hair on fire (*no one can do that with their mind; it has to be a projector hidden in the wall, right?*) drove her. At slumber parties, she concentrated all of her energy on picturing herself on stage cradling an armload of gleaming awards engraved with her accolades (Best Actress, Best Director, Best Rock Star Ever) until the other girls grew tired of staring at a blank wall. Sweat lined her temples and made her balled fists clammy as she fantasized about this or that floppy-haired boy in her favourite bands, but no pop stars ever appeared when other eyes were watching. Aggie started to think of what she could do as an involuntary twitch, something that only happened when she didn't want it to.

She tried again only once, with Van. As they sat in his basement watching a movie she wasn't really watching because she was busy wondering if he was going to kiss her or if she should kiss him, Aggie let her mind wander to the time she watched through the crack in his bedroom door as he was changing his shirt. She pictured the puff of his lower lip, his pale nipples tiny and velvety as kitten noses pricked in the cold air, the smattering of dark hair across his chest, the indentation that marked his hip just above the top of his jeans. She found herself flushed with a liquid burn from her chest down to her thighs and she knew if she did it now, he would be the one to see. But when the walls and the floor and the ceiling remained as blank and beige as they had always been, Aggie found herself questioning if she really wanted any of these things as much as she thought she did.

Now that she wanted the images to stop, though, they were coming more frequently. Ten days after the schoolgirl on her bedroom wall appeared, an image of a teenage girl emerged on the back of the bathroom door. Smoke and steam pushed against Aggie's face as she stepped out of the shower to find the teen who might have also been the school girl—same big dark eyes and long black hair this time slicked back into a low ponytail—staring back at her. Leaning against

149

a concrete wall, the girl wore cuffed jeans and a too-big leather jacket, round face grinning defiantly as a cigarette dangled from her lips. Behind her, spindly trees menaced power lines along a narrow street lined with food stalls and men in high-waisted pants and shiny black ducktail haircuts putting out cafe chairs.

Aggie made sure the towel was wrapped tightly around her before touching the door. "Who are you?" she whispered. "What do you want?"

The girl's smile seemed to widen under Aggie's fingertips.

~

A ggie left the teenage girl for her mother to find. She decided not to scrub her from the back of the bathroom door after she saw the photo albums.

It was a hunch that led her to pull the cumbersome, cracked plastic volumes from beneath the serving platters and never-used linens in the dining room hutch. These old photos didn't see the daylight very often, not since before her father died, back when her mother still cared about documenting everything in between the milestones. After all, she hadn't even bothered to right the Disneyland picture after Aggie turned it face-down in the bookcase, though Aggie took that as more a sign of her mother not wanting to face what was happening. They were the same in that way, allowing procrastination to turn into secrets. There was supposed to be college next year, though Aggie still hadn't told her mother that her grades weren't good enough for the scholarships she needed. She hadn't even told her mother that she'd been let go from her job at the mall.

Paging through the photo albums, Aggie could see the small differences starting to compile in front of her. There she was on the first day of kindergarten, excitedly clutching a plain metal lunchbox that she was sure had been a plastic Hello Kitty one. A photo from when she was twelve, showing off the purple hair that her mother had helped her dye, hair that was suddenly much longer than she remembered. Even a Polaroid from just two years ago—at the kitchen table glowering over her homework as her mother took a surreptitious snapshot—showed her in a crisp white button-down and a loose black necktie, two things Aggie had never owned. Looking at these old photos, she already knew what she would see when she finally turned the one of her and Van on her nightstand right side up.

"Look at this. Who is she?" Aggie asked her mother that night, placing the photo album atop her mother's empty dinner plate.

Julia swiped her napkin across her mouth and pushed the album across the table. "Aggs, *what?*"

"Here, Mom. Look." Aggie turned to the kindergarten picture and pressed her finger to the lunchbox. "And this." She did the same with the purple hair photo, and the white button-down Polaroid, and all of the ones in between. "Don't tell me they're old and deteriorating or whatever. Tell me who she is."

"What's gotten into you, kid?"

"Seriously, Mom. *Look.* It's like the Disneyland picture—they're all me, but not me. Something's happening."

Julia started to stand, but Aggie blocked her, kept driving her finger into every altered photo so that her mother was forced to look.

"You know who she is."

Julia squeezed her eyes shut, started to rub the spot between them like she often did at the start of a headache. "Oh, Aggie…We can't be sure, okay? I don't know what she looked like back then. There were no photos of her when she was a kid."

"She was on my wall, and now she's on the back of the bathroom door…I'm not even thinking about her, but there she is. What does she want, Mom?"

"It's not possible. You know what she was like, all those stories," Julia sighed, thumbing through the album pages so quickly that they made an audible crackle like the start of a fire. Her eyes grew glassy and she blinked hard. "Your grandmother wasn't raised in the jungle. She didn't have any magical powers or superhuman strength or any of those things she used to tell you about. My mother was an unhappy woman who wanted people to pay attention to her."

It didn't bring the relief Aggie expected, hearing her mother finally say it. The woman who worked in medicine, who believed in science and yet had seen with her own eyes what her daughter could do, was still dismissing even the possibility of supernatural forces in her own bloodline. Her mother, who had confessed that as a suburban teenager she was relieved when her skin lightened to resemble her father's; who openly regretted those shameful years of trying to erase her own mother, even as she still told Aggie not to listen to the old woman's stories—she was as stubborn and stoic as a stone wall, but the tears Aggie saw now were the little bit of validation she needed.

"She wants my attention—our attention," Aggie said, running her hands over her mother's slumped shoulders. "Can she do this, Mom? Can she?"

Julia dropped her face into her hands, making her voice muffled when she next spoke. "Maybe, Aggie. I don't know. I don't know."

～

Grandmother had often told Aggie how lucky she was that she had choices, that she could be anything she wanted. "You can read what you desire and speak what you desire and love or hate just the same," she had said, stooped eye-to-eye and holding her granddaughter by the shoulders as if her words were essential instruction. It wasn't like when she was growing up with dress codes and delicate expectations and the nuns who took her language, took her books and put an embroidery needle in her hand.

It wasn't just the exciting stories of scaling trees and midnight escapes that made Aggie admire her grandmother. The appreciation came long after her mother's stories of being the same age when she first discovered the differences others had always seen. How her friends' parents assumed she was adopted when they saw her with her mother. How at every new school teachers and students alike asked, "What are you?" as they scrutinized her face. How she rolled her eyes every time she recounted to Aggie a blind date who cooed at her "exoticness" and proclaimed his love of Thai food. These things that had once made Aggie sympathize with her mother now made her ache for her grandmother and the person she could have been if she hadn't been forced from one institution into another.

Maybe it would be better to let her grandmother steer for a while. Aggie thought that if even a little piece of that woman had been in Julia, her mother might have done more than look down at her shoes every time those teachers and classmates and moony-eyed suitors scrutinized her. She wouldn't have made her daughter hide what she could do. Grandmother wouldn't have cared when the other kids didn't believe she was special. She would've brought the stray cats inside, given them more than just cheap kibble. She wouldn't have fucked up school and work and any chance of a decent future. If Grandmother had the benefit of living in Aggie's time and place, she would have been proud of her desires, taken what she wanted, controlled her power and wielded it like the advantage that it was.

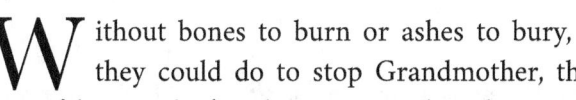

Without bones to burn or ashes to bury, there was nothing they could do to stop Grandmother, though Aggie wasn't sure if her mother's solutions were based on ancient mythology or *Buffy* reruns. After Grandmother died, her body disappeared—*a mix-up at the crematorium,* her mother had explained to family and friends —but little Aggie chose to believe that she had simply returned to the jungle, as abruptly and fully-formed as she had once appeared. If her grandmother's stories had even a little bit of truth to them, there was nothing Aggie could do but appease her mother with the shallow comfort she promised.

Luksaw, she texted her mother once again, as she had done at the top of every hour since she left for school that morning. It was this phonetically-spelled word—something Julia said Grandmother had called her when she was little, the only Thai word she had ever heard her mother speak—whispered in Aggie's ear at the breakfast table, that was supposed to let Julia know that Aggie was still herself.

"You talking to your other boyfriend?" Van teased her when she turned her phone away from his gaze.

After her mother's immediate *Thanks kid*, Aggie stuffed her phone back into her pocket and pulled the sleeves of her hoodie down over her hands. Though the sun was out, the wind made the late afternoon bitterly cold. "Have you noticed anything different about me lately?" she asked.

"Besides your ass being allergic to me?" At Aggie's eye roll, Van scooted over to the other end of the porch steps and considered her for a long moment. "Your hair. It's darker?" He lifted a section from the side of her face, before letting it slowly slide between his fingers. "And now it's straight?"

Aggie looked down at the heavy curtain of hair hanging over her t-shirt. What was once wavy and reddish brown was now stick-straight and shiny black, the perfect unbroken surface of obsidian. The same as the girl on the back of the bathroom door that her mother had spent at least an hour staring at last night before scrubbing her away.

"Yeah," she said. "You like it?"

"I love whatever you do, as long as you don't hog the bathroom all morning."

She snorted and he laughed. She was glad that he didn't seem to sense that the reason for her reaction was different this time. Sometimes she said things to make him happy, things that she assured herself she could deny later.

"You wanna do it, you really want to live together?" she asked.

Van drew his arm around Aggie and pulled her into him. She suddenly realized that she would miss this, how her head fit so perfectly in the space between his neck and shoulder. It had felt more intimate and vulnerable when her mother caught them like this, more than all the times she'd rushed down the stairs still buttoning her jeans as her mother unlocked the front door.

"Yeah, why not?" he said, his breath moving in little huffs across the top of her head. "I'm graduating and you'll be done next year too, our parents won't be able to stop us—we can go anywhere, Aggs. We don't have to stay here. We can—" He became excited, sitting up straight, letting Aggie fall from his embrace. "We can move to Thailand. Fuck this town—we'll move to Thailand! Don't you have relatives there?"

Her boyfriend's revelation made her shiver harder than the cold. "What? Van, where is this coming from?"

"Baby…" He sighed, shrugging out of his leather jacket. He placed it around Aggie's shoulders, pinching together the worn black flaps up to her chin.

"You hate the heat. You hate the beach," she continued, taking over holding the sides of the too-big jacket together from the inside. "Last summer you made me spend all of August at the movies because it was air-conditioned."

"Don't you want to go there? Don't you want to learn more about your roots?"

Her mother's regrets began to pile up in her head. Aggie had listened to the stories. She had believed. Even as she had grown older she at least *wanted* to believe. Wasn't that enough? If she got cheated now, would she get the chance to come back too?

As Van started going on about the night markets in Bangkok and snorkelling in Phuket, Aggie imagined her grandmother slowly slipping into her skin as if she were nothing more than a leotard or a wetsuit. She wondered if the changes would be gradual enough for Van, or if he would know right away and stop loving her. She wondered if her grandmother would grow to love him, or if she would feel trapped again, stuck in another situation where she was only there because she was supposed to be. Either way, Aggie thought it might not be so bad to watch from the inside, to be a passenger for a little while. Given the chance, Grandmother might make her the stronger, braver person she wanted to be.

~

"I'll always be here for you, Agnes. I'll make sure you don't make the same mistakes I did."

Grandmother only said that once in the last year of her life, though it wasn't a deathbed whisper while she clutched her granddaughter's hand. Hearing those words at thirteen, Aggie had felt the weight of her age like the first stone dropped into a pillowcase, and she took it as both warning and advice. Back then she'd feared judgement and disappointment and how easy it would be to stumble over a line that kept moving. Now, at seventeen, she was just scared.

Lying atop her bed, Aggie stared up at the newest image on her ceiling. This time her grandmother seemed to be a little older than her. She was perched on a large rock on an endless beach, dressed in shorts and a billowy t-shirt, her black hair cut short, the same as in the photo Aggie had seen on her nightstand. The photo she'd had to turn over again because she never had hair that short and she certainly hadn't worn shorts and a t-shirt to Van's sister's wedding. She shared the same blood as her grandmother, so why couldn't she be as proud and defiant? She wanted to see herself on that endless beach, feel the hot sand between her toes, find at least a piece of herself in the woman who could also do things no one understood.

Outside, the cats were starting up again. It was when Aggie was opening the window that she caught a glimpse of herself in the glass. Her hair had reverted to the soft waves she'd had her whole life. She ran to the mirror to be sure. In the harsh light of both bedside lamps and the overhead fixture, she saw her hair had faded closer to her natural reddish brown. And when she pulled down her pants, the highways of scars were no more visible than the lightest of stretch marks.

Aggie hummed as she poured the kibble, hummed to herself and the cats who didn't appreciate what this meant. The striped mother and child pair stayed close, eating together and leaving together. It was the new cat, the largest roughest one, who lingered long after the food was gone, as if he was enjoying the sound of her voice.

Luksaw, she texted her mother. The usual *Thanks kid* came before her fingers even left the keyboard.

~

V an didn't exactly say he wanted to break up, but Aggie viewed his desire to be "just friends" as just that. This sudden change in their relationship was especially strange coming from a boy who had listed "Xbox" and "sex" as his two favourite activities on their last career guidance form, so Aggie figured he had been driven away by how her grandmother had changed her. It wasn't until Van came over just before graduation that she realized the changes were all him.

"So you're really doing it," Aggie said, restlessly folding the t-shirt he'd returned over one arm then the other. This was the shirt she'd left at his house when they first started dating, when there hadn't been time to get it back on under her sweater. It was the shirt that she had let him keep because he said it smelled like her and she liked to imagine what he did with it when he was alone. Now it just smelled of Tide.

"Yeah, I got my ticket," Van said. "It's not too late for you too."

"Maybe I should go with you. The irony is my ass healed—I'm not allergic to you anymore." Aggie forced a little laugh, though it wasn't enough to change the quizzical look on her ex's face and the strange discomfort that was now settling between them.

Van reached for her, his hand landing awkwardly on her shoulder. As they stood facing each other in the middle of the living room, Aggie was surprised that she felt nothing as his hand slid down the length of her arm and away from her. She had gone from spending a week restraining herself from texting him everything that had happened with her grandmother to praying that he didn't touch her when she first opened the door. Now his presence held none of the electricity or anticipation it once had; it was as if enough time had passed for her ex-boyfriend to become pleasantly vague, as benign and familiar as a Christmas letter cousin.

"You should come," he said, and it sounded to Aggie that he meant it, separate rooms and all.

She shook her head. "I think my mom wants to go with you. She can't believe you're getting there before her."

"I'm old. I gotta go soon, while I can still enjoy it," Julia agreed as she dashed down the stairs with her laptop under her arm. "Hey, Van." She flashed a smile at him as she passed, making sure to turn so that only Aggie saw her raised eyebrow. "You all packed? You got your passport, right?"

"Yep, all ready to go."

"Good boy."

Aggie and Van stifled a giggle as they watched her mother sit down at the kitchen table with her computer and a notepad. *Good boy*, Aggie mouthed, reaching up on tiptoes to pat the top of his head. He caught her hand on the way down and she let him lock his fingers with hers, a loose grip that ended after a hard swing, the kind of hand-holding that she had done with childhood girlfriends.

"Here," Julia said, holding out a piece of paper towards Van as she crossed back into the living room. "That's my cousin in Bangkok. You can email her if you need any recommendations or if you get into trouble. But you're not—"

Van and Aggie both stared expectantly at her mother, watching Julia's mouth hang open, her wide eyes narrowing after she stopped short. She seemed both pained and fascinated as she took a couple of steps back from her daughter's ex, letting her eyes travel up and down his body twice before landing on his face again. Her pinched, scrutinizing look remained when she next spoke. "Van, you look….Did you…?"

"I won't get into any trouble, Julia, I promise." He smiled and tucked the paper into his pocket.

Laughing a little, she shook her head, trance just as suddenly broken. "I'm seeing things," she said, and both her and Aggie's eyes drifted to the bookcase by the door where the Disneyland picture still lay face-down. "I'm not senile yet, okay?" She turned back to Aggie, forcing a grin, then grabbed her computer and headed back upstairs.

"Sorry, my mom's crazy," Aggie sighed.

"Don't worry about your mom—she'll be okay."

Aggie took a step back from Van and eyed him the way her mother had. "What is going on with you?"

He lifted a section of her hair and twisted the strands into a rope, studying it for a moment before letting it drop back against her shoulder. She thought he might comment on how her hair had lightened, but all he said was, "It's okay to let people see what you want sometimes."

"Van…?"

Aggie didn't need to finish because she saw it then. In the hazy afternoon sunlight that filtered through the blinds, she could see that his light brown hair had darkened and the always slouched curve of his back had straightened as if he was now proud of all six feet and two inches. She could picture him leaning against a concrete wall outside a night market in his too-big leather jacket, a cigarette and a defiant grin on his lips.

"I gotta go," Van said, offering her a sad little smile as he turned towards the door. "Think about going, okay? Seriously."

"Sure."

Aggie walked behind him to the door and opened it, but he stopped just short of walking through. Her shoulders stiffened as he turned around, even though his hands were now stuffed in his pockets.

"If you need anything...I'll always be here for you, Agnes. I'm not making those mistakes again."

Aggie squeezed the t-shirt she'd been holding this whole time in both fists, felt her own cold sweat mix with the fresh perspiration that had started again on her palms. As they said their goodbyes, she thought of the orphanage and the nuns and the jungle and the cobras making their wide arc. She thought of the schoolgirl, the midnight escapes, the woman on the beach who lost herself even before someone else's time and place took her. She thought of the picture of herself and Van on her nightstand, and she knew what she would see this time when she turned it over.

WAKING FIRE

I.J.P. RUIZ

By Golden Cord, Apolaki reigned; alone in pride and will.

Then Mayari rose for her right to rule; in shock, the sun god stilled.

When he refused, she drew her club, and their strikes shook the sky.

'til Apolaki, in fury's haze, struck out his sister's eye.

Ashamed, he vowed he'd rule the day; with silver she'd be crowned.

So ever since she reigns the night, dimmed, but uncowed.

Such were my dreams, where father's stories burst to life with tales of the Diwata, our ancestor's gods. Its here that I saw that cord of gold, over and over, its light blazing like new year's fireworks. Even from my dorm in the capital, it burned my sleep. Even as I tried to forget it, it called me home.

My home, *Espiritu Cresta*, bounds the edge of a volcanic lake, its hills and shores no strangers to legends. In the time of Rajahs and Datus, the land was hallowed ground; a place of shrines and homes to our old gods. Yet like many other things, they were swept aside by Spanish might, pagan shrines demolished to make way for churches and barracks. What could be moved was plundered, anything that could not was simply destroyed. Yet even now, these treasures are not lost to the initiated. Those with the dedication, connections, and buyers could thrive. And so my father, Omarion Tupas, "Mar" to his friends, set up shop in an old Spanish chapel not long after I was born – yet his reasons for settling here ran deeper than love of the past.

An oath is like a rope well tied, no matter how taut, it shall not loose or fray – this was Mar's bond with the Covenant. With a name like that, I thought they were merely some obscure Catholic order, but from what I saw, I began to doubt. They paid his bills under a variety of false names and addresses. By father's network of courier and dealers, relics passed through his shop at a breathtaking pace. But to what end? Reports arrived with facts and figures—snippets of local myths, rare antiques, anything to support his mysterious obsession. Yet while father never hid his work from me, all questions of what and why were laid aside, the first flame lit beneath the kettle of my frustrations.

By age 17, I was already tired of the secrets. I booked the first coach out of town, off to university in the capital. Father sent me off with tears in his eyes, his lonely frame withered as the coach pulled out. Blinking back my own tears, I forced myself to turn away.

Two years of study passed with little more than the odd text from father. His old friend, Reinaldo Cabatingan, or Uncle "Rein", became Mayor shortly after I left, and what I heard made me glad I was gone.

"FOR LAW AND ORDER" his slogan read, a claim as audacious as the man himself. He made the barangay councilors his courtiers, the police became his personal militia, and his enemies disappeared like thieves and traitors. A ruthless Datu for the modern age had risen, and no one in the capital seemed to care. Imagine my shock when his men appeared on my doorstep. Built like carabao, their glares brooked no protest - I was going home.

We drove along the highway to *Espiritu*, "the Road to the Sky." Its course took us from the sprawling bustle of the plains, up through the winding hills and plantations. The others kept to themselves, leaving me to my mounting dread. Only a day before, my biggest worry was registering for study-abroad. What did father get himself into?

I didn't recognize home at first. Instead of battered jeepneys, socialites drove by in gleaming D-Maxes and imported Porsches. Elegant estates rose on once empty hill tops and star-eyed crowds walked on newly paved side-walks, marveling at the lake below. A motor bike squeezed and weaved to get ahead, barely missing a young peddler piled high with chicharron and peanuts. By the next traffic light, the Mayor's guards were on him, hauling him off his bike and onto the curb. A part of me marveled at the transformation, but what was the cost?

～

After two years without seeing my father, the first thing I noticed was the grey. It was as if someone had injected grey into every part of him; from his hair, to his very skin. Then my heart sank as I looked about the warehouse, among precious relics and antiques, were bags of white powder and an arsenal of weapons.

And so the Mayor "persuaded" the brilliant antiquarian to serve him: a unique asset in his smuggling empire as it spread its reach across the province. Even father's Covenant 'friends' turned away. Gone were the funds, reports and couriers. Only the next crate mattered, the next shipment of death. So with each box I sealed, I uttered a prayer to their future victims for forgiveness, one sleepless night at a time.

On such nights, I found comfort in passing my hands through a candle flame. In time, the passes grew longer, the number of candles grew, and the heat's intensity waned. Eventually I taught myself some-thing that made father's eyes widen in wonder: how to pass the flame along my fingers, from one candle to the next.

Weeks after my return, the past came back to me in father's office.

Against the wall, between two worn bookshelves, was a 19th century

163

bargueño desk that had seen better days. Inlayed with tarnished metal, it must have been beautiful long ago. For every faded vignette of sails against a distant horizon, there was an image of the conquered, bound in chains of iron and faith. Nowhere in our shop could you find a more fitting tribute to the glory and hubris of *Monarquía Hispánica*. In retrospect, there way a charming irony to how this piece of history would preserve another.

Within was the Golden Cord; the one that shadowed my dreams. As a child, I found it while father and Uncle Rein traded laughs on shop floor, echoes of happier times. The adventure games I once played taught me that old things always held hidden secrets. Amused by my logic, father suggested that I start my search here. To this day, I don't know if he was teasing or testing me. Soon enough, my fumbling shifted one of the panels, revealing a recess no longer than my forearm, cut into the wall behind the desk.

Inside was a glowing crystal set into a stone much older than the wall around it. The golden light from within took the hazy shape of the Cord. My hand rose to touch its face and a six-winged crest appeared, as if carved into the shard itself. Warm to the touch, I could not shake the sense of familiarity. When I removed my hand and shuffled back, it dimmed once more. My mind raced. Even at that age, I could tell I found something special.

When I stood up, I saw the smartest man I knew in his prime. Lanky and gallant in stride, Father's eyes twinkled with mirth. Uncle Rein used to put him in such a good mood.

"Any treasures, Josal?" he asked.

Excited, I showed him what I found. As I repeated my actions, he picked them over with his eyes, taking in every detail. Even after I finished, he was silent, as if he was turning over my words in his head.

It was the first time my abilities gave him pause, the first of many times to come.

∾

A week before the full moon, I found myself struggling with another shipment of contraband. As I cursed manifests, I heard voices from the shop floor.

"The Mayor sends his best, uncle." I knew that voice too well.

Fearing the worst, I crept to the corner without a sound. Peeking between the furniture and old statues on display, father stood cornered by a familiar face. It was Ronnie Cabatingan, Uncle Rein's son, and his cadre of armed guards.

"And ours to him. Are you here to give me feedback on another shipping problem?" Father was terse, leaning heavily on his left leg. The right was still healing from last month's 'feedback session.'

"Not today. I was passing by and thought I should deliver the news in person." A hollow smile curled beneath Ronnie's empty eyes, sunken into a reddish web of burns that never faded with the passage of time.

"According to this week's manifest, a shipment is coming in on the night of the full moon. My father has seen pictures of the piece coming in. He's happy to take it off your hands. I will be coming at 8:15pm to make the pickup."

"But the original client is…"

"Taken care of. Father believes such a fine relic will fetch a handsome price. Its value in cash will be put to better uses- the cause of rebuilding this damn broken country, piece by piece. He will turn it into something we can believe in, and I will not tolerate any mistakes that get in our way. Have I made myself clear?"

My father nodded, and Ronnie left without a word. When I emerged, asking him what happened, he simply sobbed, as I held his withered hand.

As father composed himself, I reopened the bargueño hoping that age and experience would tell me more than father ever could. Opening the compartment as I did many years before, I peered into the crystal once more.

The sight was clearer than I remember. What looked like a rope from afar, was really strings of fine threaded beads, row upon row weaved together. It was fastened in a loop at one end and the other end had a cap to prevent fraying. Every part shone with a golden gleam. Accessories were not my area of expertise at the time, but it seemed more fitting on a Hindu deva than a Spanish lord.

Then it clicked in my head. Turning to the bookshelves, I quickly scanned the spines. At university and since my return, I spent many hours deep in the shelves. After a while, the same names come up, no matter what field you study. *Bernini, Berruguete, Borlase, Boxer!*

I pulled out our copy of the Boxer Codex, and there it was on the cover - a drawing of a tagalog warrior in red robes, with a golden cord draped over his shoulder. It's a Maharlika's sash...

"Its real name is the *Cord of the Sun*. Your practice is really paying off."

Father returned. Even in the face of crisis he was as cryptic as ever. Concern melted away, and frustration returned full force, threatening to boil over.

"What's so important about it?" I returned the codex to its proper place before turning back to him. "Does the shipment have something to do with it?"

Father was silent. He never lied. Instead, he would refuse to acknowledge what he did not want to say. Another aspect of him I admired and resented. Like many times before, he placed his hand on my shoulder and tried to wave it off.

"No, its too late. It doesn't matter now," he said.

I shoved his hand away. "WHY NOT?!"

"All my life, you've been searching for something right under your nose! For people I don't know, and reasons I don't understand!

Are you trying to protect me? 'Cause that's working out great! I'm trapped by a drug lord who could kill us in a week, and I won't have a damn idea why!

What's stopping you?!"

Out of air, I took several breaths, my glare never leaving his face. He stared past me, as if under a spell.

After what felt like hours, he replied, "What do you want to know?"

"Why's the Cord such a big deal?"

"Its an artifact of the old gods; just like the stories I told you," he began. "My order, the Covenant, has known about its hiding place for years. Beneath us is a shrine dedicated to Apolaki, God of War and Sun. A Jesuit priest risked it all to save it during the first waves of colonization, building this chapel around it.

As the centuries past, the Order saw no reason to move the crystal, or to try and retrieve it. Without the right key, it was safer where it was, as long as a guardian like me kept it safe.

The rise of the Cabatingans changed the scales. This legacy of the gods can't fall into their hands. Since then, the Covenant has been working out a plan..."

A fortnight ago, father received a coded message. The Covenant had figured out a way to retrieve the Cord, with a second diwata relic. With the logistics worked out, it was on its way, disguised as an ordinary shipment. Everything was going according to plan until the Mayor decided he wanted it himself.

"What took them so long?" It was the first time we had explicitly discussed the Covenant and I was incensed. They were more concerned with sending things in, rather than smuggling him out.

He smiled sadly. "It's not that simple. There's a 'presence' in the air here. It listens and intercepts all our communications, and allows nothing to leave town unless the Cabatingans want it to. But there's still a chance that something can come in if it's something they are expecting.

If we had more time, the second artifact could have worked by itself over a few days. We wouldn't need the main key: You."

"Me?"

"Apolaki sleeps within you, Josal. He dreams of the cord that is his duty and birthright, locked away long ago. Once reunited, he will be whole again."

My head swam, a decade of doubt washed away. If I hadn't asked for the truth, I wouldn't have believed any of this.

"Well I'm right here! Why won't it unseal for me right now?"

"Lack of power," he said. "You've only tasted a hint of what you can wield. Once unlocked, you'll have what you need to set all of us free…"

∽

Leading up to the big night, my thoughts turned to the truth of father's world.

Whatever the Covenant was, it seems to have diminished over the years. If I was younger, I'd have imagined father as a secret agent; one who jet-setted across the world and foiled the machinations of laughing madmen with a quick wit and sharp aim, leaving the real world ignorant to the near-triumph of a great evil. But the truth was always more messy. Sometimes the Covenant did not receive his messages. Sometimes their intelligence was wrong. Sometimes he struggled to make the cheques last from one month to the next delayed payment. And since the Cabatingans came to power we had barely heard from them. He was a prisoner. They seemed powerless to help him. All the dreams I had of invulnerable secret societies vanished. In the real world they operated in shadows, while their informants, like father, remained trapped wherever they stayed.

168

Meanwhile, Ronnie, who hid behind the gates of the mansion after he was burned, appeared around town more than ever; inhuman, emotionless. I tried to remember the boy I once played with, when Reinaldo father was not a minor warlord but a pious man and father's dearest friend. When they discussed the history of our islands, the severed threads to our past, and the nature of God himself. In those meetings, the man who would be mayor slammed his fists on the table in determination, swearing change would come by his hand. Now they seemed locked in their own world, distant strangers converging on us. A world run by wealth and power, sparked by a single loose firework. I thought of that night again and again as the full moon drew closer.

We were kids basking under the blossoming display, trails of fire whizzed into the humid darkness, and burst into hot contrails of light. With a trip and a spark, a rogue firework shot Ronnie's way. Without a second thought, I threw myself in its path – and my world was consumed by fire. Never before had I suffered worse pain than those third-degree burns, but it was worth it as long as Ronnie survived.

Even though I caught most of the blast, both of us suffered for months. Yet as all my scars miraculously healed, Ronnie's scars worsened. Whether it was out of resentment or shame, he never told me why he pushed me away.

~

Sunset. The night of the full moon. Above Piña Lake, in a ring of ritual stones, I re-read father's instructions, copied from notes the Covenant provided.

Stand at the top of the ridge with a clear view of the lake.

Raise the club to the moon until it glows.

Draw the club across the ground in a circle at your feet.

. . .

I wrestled with the knot in my stomach. Every time I went over father's plan, the knot only grew tighter.

Once the ritual was complete, I had to run back and return the club before Ronnie and his men arrived. Once I had performed the ritual we would have the power to free the Cord, and make our escape. Beyond that, there were no further instructions. *What then? How would we leave town? Where would we take the Cord?* The Covenant left these questions unanswered.

Before long, the sun dipped beneath the horizon.

I reached for the long case I carefully hauled up during the climb, and popped it open. Within was the treasure the Mayor so desired: a hefty ironwood war club with an octagonal cut shaft and a hand-carved grip. Though well crafted, it looked no different from other relic weapons I'd seen in my work. I admit, it was a bit of a letdown. Brushing off the disappointment, I checked the skies.

Where clouds often obscured the stars, an empty sky let the moon shine through, lonely and beautiful. Still and quiet. My breathing slowed, and I let the tension drain away. Suddenly I wasn't even thinking. I felt the old god stir within, and I could do nothing to resist.

By instinct I raised the club high, and let flames crackle from my hands. In moonlight, the club's true nature was revealed: Baybayin, our ancient pre-hispanic script, lined the club's shaft. In seconds, rustic brown gave way to silvery white, casting a cool glow across the hilltop. In my grasp was another figment of my dreams: the War Club of Mayari.

Pulsing with anticipation, I drew the club in a ring around me. The curve filled with light as it passed. When I completed the circle, the ground shuddered, and the world flashed white. Overwhelmed, I closed my eyes, and stood my ground until shaking stopped.

When I opened my eyes, I was in a different world.

The moon hung low against the starry night, more massive than it could ever be on Earth. It illuminated a rippling sea, stretched to the dark horizon. The only object in sight was an empty throne of silvery stonework, framed by the glare of the midnight sun.

Then the stillness shifted before the throne. The moon's reflection rose from the surface, carrying sheets of water upon it. Before my eyes, the rippling reflection swirled into the shape of a tall woman with skin of midnight skies. Robes of dark blue hung from her slight frame, and her head was crowned with locks of silver. Most striking was the light that poured through her eyes, like radiant beams through church glass. Yet despite their brightness, one eye glowed dimmer than the other.

"Mayari."

"Few of The People still know my name." Though her lips did not move, her clarion voice rang through my ears.

"Do you know my brother's? A fruit should know the tree from whence it came."

"Apolaki. I carry his power?"

"You are not the first. Who but your predecessor could set a lock, to which only you hold the key?"

Though I heard her words, I didn't grasp what she meant. As if sensing my confusion, she spelled it out.

"You are what your father serves - The Covenant incarnate. Man and god united in this life and the next; watching over an unknowing world. For to us come monsters in the dark. They pound on long-sealed doors, and their servants seek to break the locks. You know two of them well..."

In that moment, it all clicked together. Uncle Rein, Ronnie, and the blast that changed them both. My heart fell. *They chose their path*, I thought. But I could never have imagined this.

"The men you once knew are possessed. Mere instruments in a design even I cannot see. All of this the Covenant knows, thanks to your father's dedication and sacrifice. Now do you understand why you are here?"

Shame. Guilt. They welled up from my every pore. For years I had resented father and his obsession with the Covenant. At times I even questioned his sanity. I felt like such a fool.

"I do." I met her gaze. "But even with this power, how do I get us out?"

Mayari drew close, and placed a starry hand on my shoulder.

"Before I undo the chain, let me tell you my story. The parts that time forgotten. "

"Ever since the stars were young, Brother always held his age above my head. Timid and shy, I let him get his way. Every decision I made, he second-guessed. Every wonder in the sky I created was outshone by his own. Yet as we aged, father Bathala never doubted that I was Brother's equal. At the time I did not believe, dismissing his words as comfort given to a second child.

"Yet when Father passed into the great beyond, he left the throne to us both."

"Immediately brother declared that he would rule alone, betraying our father's wishes. Instead of retreating like night before dawn, I stood between him and the throne, and refused to let him pass. Never had I seen Brother's eyes grow so wide."

"Our battle shook the heavens, as the stories tell. They say it ended with the loss of my eye, as my brother looked on in pity and remorse. But the stories miss one truth. Only when I rose half-blind to strike him back did he concede. He saw what father saw my whole life, something that exceeded his own - will."

Pulling her hand from my shoulder, she placed it beneath my neck. "Carry that with you. Whether you endured years of imprisonment, fought for father's last wish, or took a blow meant for a friend, your will to rise for another is all the Covenant requires." As if she flipped a switch, a rush of power surged into my chest.

"And should you fall, do not fear. When you stand by your covenant, the Covenant stands with you."

With a single push, I fell through her world and hurtled into an endless sky.

~

My back throbbed. The earth pressed into my palms. She sent me back to the hilltop.

As I moved to brush the grass off, I was shocked by how bright my arm was. Lines of sunlight glowed on my limbs and chest. Spotting a pool of water, I scrambled to it and gasped at what I saw.

The sun god's eyes stared back, and six flaming wings flared into the skies behind. By Mayari's hand, the locks were undone! Never before had I felt so warm.

Incessant beeping cut through my elation. Despite the heat, my watch seemed to be working.

8:15!

No matter how fast I could run, I would never make it in time. Tentatively, I flexed my new wings. There was no time to doubt. I sprinted to the rim of the caldera and jumped.

Wind whipped and whistled past, but the dark hills pulled away from sight. My wings stretched out, like hands embracing the earth. *I was flying!*

Soaring, I scanned the ground for familiar signs and spotted a patchwork of lights at the edge of the lake and the street lamps lining the Road to the Sky. Effortlessly, the wings carried me home. As I drew close to a familiar roof, my blood ran cold. The chapel's lights were out, and the headlamps of an empty Jeep lit the front doors, battered in from the outside.

Descending with my eyes fixed on the shattered doors, I spotted two dark shapes in the open. Ronnie's guards had their eyes fixed on the road. Silently I fell, lowering my legs. As I descended, one of the pair saw the light descending on him and turned too late. Beneath my feet they fell to earth, out cold without a sound.

I clutched Mayari's club tight, as I rushed forth through the doors, praying that I wasn't too late.

"I am only going to ask one more time uncle - where are Joseph and the club?"

I heard a punch and grunt of pain from the back office. In the doorway I saw Ronnie's back. He towered over father, whose face throbbed purple and red. His cane lay splintered behind him.

"Is that desperation, demon?" He gasped with pain. "I didn't think your kind were capable of emotion beyond insufferable confidence. Josal is beyond you, and your father's reach!" He sat up against the bargueño, leaning to support his battered body. "So by all means, linger here. I've helped enough monsters like you to damn me for a thousand lifetimes. Its time you did something yourself for a change!"

"I do want to kill you, uncle. But even lesser beings like you have a use." Ronnie rolled back his sleeve. Where an arm should be, a viscous black mass writhed in its place. "If you no longer wish to be a pawn, then you shall serve as a skin for my brothers..."

The mass reformed into a needle and he raised this to father's forehead. Father glared in defiance, ready. That was it. Despite knowing Ronnie was in there, rage surged through every nerve. The creature that took my friend would never take my father.

Like a volcano on eruption's edge, fire roiled from my chest, to Mayari's club. Stepping from my hiding place, I leveled it at Ronnie's head, and let it go

Sunfire roared with the force of a rocket, forcing me to my knees.

174

Half blind and arm sizzling, it took all I had to stop the club flying from my white knuckled grip.

When the last of the blast bled away, I pitched sideways and hit the floor hard. , the stench of burning flesh stabbed my nostrils. Sickened, I heaved but there was nothing to throw up. Gasping, I opened my eyes to see little more than flickering blobs in the dark. My eyes stung

"Father!" For a moment, no sound rose above the crackling flames. Had I incinerated him too? Then I heard a hoarse cough. Still half blind, I scrambled towards it on all fours, until the white of father's smile beamed through the blur. "I knew you would make it."

"I had to," blindly, I felt for his face, and struggled to suppress a sob. "I'm glad you're still here."

I hugged him, longer and tighter than I've held anyone in my life. Though father's breath was shallow and pained, he was still breathing. As my hug slacked, father spoke again. "You got a good hit. But you've only slowed it down. Grab the Cord so we can get out of here..."

"What! Slowed?! He's..."

"Fire isn't enough," he gasped. "Hurry!"

Through bleary eyes, I saw 'Ronnie' twitch and ooze a dark violet mist. It folded messily onto itself and collapsed into black sludge. In seconds, a new shape began to rise.

Pressing my hand against the charred desk, I opened the hidden panel and reached straight through the glowing crystal. When I pulled it out, the Cord glowed in my grip. Slinging it like a sash across one of my shoulders, I looped Father's good arm around my neck and helped him to his feet. As we hurried to the back door, he raised a watch that I had never seen before to his face.

"Selene! This is Assisi! Get us out of here!"

Only a few steps out the front, we ran out of time. The wall shattered, the blast throwing us both to the curb. Coughing dust, I pushed off the debris and tried to get my bearings. Though the Cord was still around my shoulders, the club had disappeared among the ruins. There was no time to search. Stumbling to stand between father and the ruins, I turned to face the creature.

A mutilated mockery of Ronnie stood among the wreckage. Rushing forward, it seized me with oozing claws. Half-dead from exhaustion, I tried to pry its talons from my neck. I kicked, writhed and even tried to reignite myself, but I had released too much too soon.

Too tired.

Too weak.

As I struggled to breathe, I began to slip away as it reached for the Cord. In the haze, father yelled for help.

Gunfire answered.

Tracer rounds riddled the creature's head. Reeling, it shrieked and dropped me to the ground. Gasping for air, I turned. Who took the shot? When I saw them rush forward, my spirits soared. A dozen commandos clad in black surged out of the night. Tracer rounds shot forth from assault rifles, and radiant power streaked from staves of light. And amid the charging soldiers stood father, urging them forward. *The Covenant! The Covenant had come!*

It was all too much for the creature. Under their firepower, the thing withered and collapsed to the ground. Though violet blood gushed from every wound, it didn't die. Folding in on itself, it morphed itself into a black dog, and scampered into the night, leaving a mauled body behind.

To my shock, the body's chest lightly rose and sank. Cautious, I dragged myself closer, until a single eye met my gaze.

"Sal…" A nickname from a more innocent time.

At that old nickname of mine, all doubts melted away. "I'm here, Ronnie!"

None of his limbs were intact. One leg was bent the wrong way. The other lay behind his head. The rest of him was burned; broken beyond recognition.

"You did it…" He managed a weak smile. "I'm free…"

"Don't talk, Ron. You're going to be fine." I held his one good hand tight. "They can save you…" Crimson poured from wounds too many to count.

"You… already have," he winced. "Thank you for saving me… one last time."

His eye slid shut. I knew he was gone.

Lost to the world, I clung to his hand and wept. Past that, I remember no more.

~

It had been five nights since Ronnie died a free man. After an airlift by helicopter and a flight by private jet, I sat in one of the finest hospitals in Singapore; far from the Mayor's reach.

Peeking into my father's private ward, I suppressed a chuckle. Even in bed, he was putting on a show of good health for one of his nurses. While his spirit had not been injured by the fight, I couldn't say the same for his body. Even beneath clean bandages he still looked like he had been tied to a truck and dragged down a backwater road.

Looking back, I still marvel that either of us made it out alive. The shapeshifter defied nature and sanity with every step. Even now, I shudder at the thought of its claws viced around my neck. Even now, hate flares at the suffering it put Ronnie through. Yet even as I mourned, there was grim satisfaction in knowing that I mauled the creature that took his life, and the lives of so many others. Covenant agents were already in the field trying to pick up its trail. Whatever the creature was planning, it had to be stopped.

After the nurse finished her tests, she left to give us privacy. Father waved me over and I pulled up a chair. For a few moments, we sat in silence. This was the first time since arriving that we were alone. After what felt like many minutes, he spoke first, meeting my gaze with weathered eyes.

"I'm sorry son. For everything I didn't say.

The Covenant swears its agents to secrecy, for reasons which you're now aware. But I never realized how much it ate away at you. I think it's a little miracle that you even agreed to do the ritual, even after so many things went wrong." He looked wistfully out the window, watching an Angsana gently sway in the breeze. "Obsession got the better of me. Made me forget what really matters…"

I shook my head. "This work is more important than anyone. Even I can see that now."

"In service to a goddess, protecting our past, No wonder the Covenant moved mountains to get you back." I knew I'd have gotten in the way if I knew sooner. I placed my hand on his own. "I'm proud of you too. I'm glad to be your son."

Father nodded, tearful relief plain on his face. He composed himself.

"And what do you think of our new Covenant friends?"

I paused for a moment, thinking over everything that happened. It was hard to believe I'd been trapped for just shy of a year.

"I don't know what to say. Their resource, your mission, the fact that you help living gods...

There's no way I could go back out there - knowing all this. And I'm sure that the Covenant wouldn't just let me walk. Where do I go from here?"

"I know the feeling. I've walked in the shadows for almost 20 years and I still don't understand half of the things I've seen. But if there's one thing the Covenant has strived to do right, through all the ages of history. In the end, they try to give all of us a choice." Father pressed a button on the bed frame. Seconds later, a guard came in with a briefcase and handed it me. With a sharp salute to father, we were left alone once more.

Father nodded with encouragement. I undid the locks and lifted the lid. My eyes widened at the familiar light of Apolaki's Cord.

"The rules are simple. Since restoring Apolaki, he resides in you. However, he may also return to his Cord.

Up to a week after your powers awaken, you can pass him to another person or item, once."

Father broke down my options. "If you return him, you may join the Covenant as I have. You will be assessed for useful skills, aptitudes, and experience, then offered fitting positions. Just as I have done, you can help protect the world from the unnatural."

"If you return him and do not choose the Covenant, you will return to normal life with a new name and a fresh start. Your future is yours to choose, but your past will be rewritten so that no trace of your time with the Covenant remains. Even your memories of me will be erased."

"Finally, you may let the week elapse. After that week, Apolaki's soul will be joined to yours unto death – a Covenant for a lifetime. You will be trained to master your gifts, and work with many others just like you. Should you finish your training, you will be the tip of the spear in our secret war to keep this world turning. And I will be with you every step of the way.

Any questions?"

Smiling, I shook my head, and sealed the case. I had already decided.

UNVEILING THE NIGHT

SERAH LOUIS

Arya bent in front of the mirror, her forehead creased in concentration as she applied the dark red liquid lipstick. It wasn't normally a colour she would wear—her friends often affectionately mocked her for her customary all-black ensembles and minimalistic makeup—but Roni insisted. Arya couldn't deny her best friend on her birthday.

Roni cursed under her breath as she struggled to pull on her ripped skinny jeans. Arya glanced at her friend's reflection with amusement. "Told you they were too tight."

"They'll fit," Roni muttered between gritted teeth, and, with a final victorious tug, she surveyed her rear in the mirror with approval. "I just won't be able to eat anything till we get back."

Arya pursed her lips, putting away the lipstick. Roni was right, the colour suited her dark, dewy skin, and nicely offset her clean, pulled-back hairstyle.

"You look hot, Arya," Roni commented, adjusting the thin straps of her red halter from behind.

"Ma would probably pass out if she saw me right now."

Arya felt little guilt. Her relationship with her conservative family was tenuous at best—a father who mostly ignored her existence and doted upon her younger brother, a mother who warned her about "indecent" Western norms and bemoaned the dusky hue of her skin, and an aunt who seemed to be under the impression she was the devil incarnate.

She did love her brother, who had remained remarkably wholesome, despite his coddling, and her paternal grandmother, who cheerfully assisted in many a nightly escapade. As a child, Arya had been regaled by her grandmother's or Achamma's theatrical bedtime tales of the gods and goddesses, demons and humans. While her parents believed her grandmother was imparting good Hindu morals, Achamma had secretly entertained Arya with detailed descriptions of gore and romance.

"Live your life, child," Achamma had patted her hand solemnly that evening, speaking in her native Malayalam, "But don't rat me out to your parents." That was the Golden Rule. Achamma would never overtly take a stand against her parents, but clearly had few qualms over going behind their backs.

Anyway, Arya reasoned, she was twenty years old and even worked part-time. Her job as an assistant self-defence instructor didn't pay enough to fully cover her university expenses – a factor that her parents continually reminded her of. They couldn't understand why she didn't apply for a position at her father's hospital or something more—to quote her aunt—"ladylike." After all, her mother lamented, Arya's muscular arms would never draw her a husband.

"Ready?" Roni grabbed her clutch and opened the front door of her small apartment flat, rummaging for her keys.

Arya took one final glance at her reflection: the long swathe of dark hair, the large eyes accentuated with black eyeliner, the crimson full-lips, and the subtle shimmer of highlighter on her dark skin. She pushed away the latent insecurities, her mother's pitying tone, the childhood bullies, and the condescending relatives.

T hey reached the club downtown at midnight.

They pulled out their driver's licenses methodically, handing them to the bouncer at the entrance. While he verified their birthdates, Arya's attention was momentarily diverted by one of the bouncers inside, who was staring at them vacantly. His bald head gleamed under the low light and he filled almost the entire doorway with his broad, muscular frame. His black T-shirt bared his toned arms, which were almost completely obscured by sleeve tattoos. Under the dim lighting, the ink almost seemed to snake under his skin.

"You can go in," the bouncer grunted, handing them their licenses, and when Arya turned back to the doorway, the tattooed bouncer seemed to have disappeared further inside.

She followed Roni up the narrow staircase, already wincing at the volume of the music. The circular room was crammed with a mesh of writhing bodies, moving at a discordant pace to the rhythm of the song. It was excessively warm; the air was sticky and sweaty bodies brushed up against her with every movement she made. Roni grabbed her hand and pulled her into the midst of the crowd, laughing at Arya's disgruntled expression. "C'mon, Arya, dance!"

Her friend shimmied up to a red-headed girl on her right, laughing in delight at something the girl had said. Arya shook her head, smiling, and began to dance as well, closing her eyes briefly to pretend there was no one else in the room.

When she opened her eyes, Roni had vanished. The red-head remained, casting her a sultry glance under heavily-lidded eyes. Arya saw only unfamiliar faces. She pushed her way out, back to the front of the room, but Roni was not there either. She felt a sharp sort of panic stab at her, but she forced herself to calm down. Pulling out her phone, she sent Roni a swift message, and strode down the edge of the bar, ignoring the stares and the occasional catcall. *Washroom,* she decided, Roni must have decided to go to the washroom. She would never leave Arya on her own.

She found a second set of stairs leading to the basement with a sign indicating the washrooms were below. She took a deep breath and headed down; it was darker and quieter, though she could discern people moving around. She checked her phone again, but her friend had not responded. She entered the small, dank bathroom, lined with a row of stalls.

The music almost masked the soft cries in the last stall, but not quite.

"Are you okay?" Arya raised her voice, warily approaching the dark end of the room. The lights flickered eerily and there was a sharp bang that made her startle.

"Leave us alone, will you?" A rough male voice grunted.

She felt heat creep up her cheeks but she couldn't push away the uncomfortable sensation that something was not quite right.

Pulling out her phone, she decided to call her friend. She paused when she heard a ringtone from the stall. She strode back over to the bathroom stall at the end, knocking on it sharply. "Roni!"

"Get the fuck out, what's wrong with you?" the man inside screeched, but she continued to hit the door.

"Let her out now!" she screamed, her stomach roiling with a mixture of fear and anger; she could see the outline of her friend's black heels under the door, "Do you want me to call the bouncers or the cops?"

At once, the door flung open, and the man strode out, his face a shadowed mask of contorted fury. He was clearly only a few years older than her, with his unlined facial features and full head of blonde hair. He loomed over her menacingly, raking her figure. Roni was behind him, her hair a tangled nest and her jeans unbuttoned, loosely slung around her waist.

"You fucking pervert," Arya hissed, before turning to her friend. "Roni, come out of there, love." Roni took a few cautious steps forward, but the man advanced on Arya menacingly.

"What did you say to me?" he whispered, backing her into the sink behind, his beady eyes intensely fixated upon her, "You'd call the cops? The bouncers?"

Arya pushed at him roughly. "I'm calling them right now." She lifted her knee to hit him in the groin, but he was ready, shoving her back with his hand clenched over her leg tightly. "Roni, get someone!" she screamed, but her friend seemed frozen in space.

Arya clawed at the man's face, trying to reach his cold eyes, but he did nothing except grin and grab her wrist. Adrenaline kicked in, and she struggled, momentarily forgetting her training in a simple, instinctive urge to free herself. His callused hand that had previously been gripping her knee only slid further up her leg and she launched herself forward instead, biting down on his hand hard, drawing blood. He let go of her hand, cursing, and punched her jaw with considerable force. She gasped, her vision blurring. She tasted blood.

A tattoo of a snake crawled up his inner arm as he yanked her head back by her hair. "You should have listened when I told you to leave," he spat.

Arya screamed. Not from fear. But with fury. Primitive. Violent.

"So you lied to us, betrayed our trust and snuck out at midnight from this house?" her father asked, his fingers steepled together in a semblance of tranquillity, as he sat in his black armchair. Her mother and aunt formed a pair of sentinels behind him, glaring at her in their matching floral nightgowns.

Arya nodded, her arms folded, "I'm sorry."

"No, you're not," he replied calmly, scratching his greying beard with solemnity, "You say those words, but do you truly mean them?"

She shifted her gaze away, "The important thing was that I was there for Roni when –"

"This is all because of that girl!" her mother piped in disapprovingly, "I always knew she would land you in trouble, she's a bad one, she is. Always hopping from one boy to the next, completely bereft of culture and values, *drinking*, what self-respecting girl…"

Arya patiently waited for her mother's rant to end; she knew very well she would not listen to reason.

"…and those clothes! She told you to wear these…indecent things, did she?" Her mother gestured at Arya's scarlet ensemble with her thin lips pursed.

Arya deftly avoided the topic. "Can we please discuss what's important here? My best friend was sexually harassed –"

"I'm not surprised," her aunt murmured silkily, "If that's the way she behaves and dresses, you both were at a *club*, no less, what man wouldn't –"

"Are you seriously blaming Roni for what happened?"

"Sit down," her father ordered between gritted teeth, "Don't speak to your *Ammayi* that way, girl."

"I'm sorry, but how is this right?" she questioned in a softer tone, attempting to guise her anger, "This is the whole problem with your mentality, how can you blame the victim, and say she was asking for it? Just because she's a woman?"

"And you got the police involved too, they'll be coming in to question you tomorrow and what will we tell the neighbours when they ask?" her mother wrung her hands.

Two policemen had arrived at the club and dropped both her and Roni off at their respective homes. Arya had hoped to make a swift silent entry back into her bed, but her mother had apparently seen them arrive in the police car from the window. She had intercepted Arya at the door with a series of incensed inquiries in Malayalam.

"I told you," her aunt sniffed scornfully, "You give her too much freedom."

"I'm really tired," Arya ignored her aunt. "Can we please resume this in the morning?"

The door creaked open and they swivelled around. Achamma appeared with masterful timing.

"What's happening here? Why are you all awake?"

"Did we wake you?" her mother asked apologetically, "It's nothing, go back to sleep."

"With your incessant caterwauling, I find that will be highly unlikely," the elderly woman snapped with a deceptively sweet smile. Arya could have sworn her grandmother winked at her before she gestured, "Come, dear, do you mind helping me back to my room?"

Arya leaped up. "Of course, Achamma." She took her grandmother's wrinkled brown hand and escorted her out of the living room. They walked in silence to the room at the end of the hall. It was the smallest but coziest room in the house, with a twin-sized bed engulfed by a quilted blanket and a bookcase littered with chronicles on Hindu lore, stacked precariously in tottering piles. Bronze effigies of the gods and goddesses stood guard on the highest shelf, staring down at her sternly. The electric heater at the corner of the room spewed puffs of hot air.

Arya closed the door behind them, glancing at her grandmother, who abruptly dropped the façade of elderly exhaustion and plopped down on her bed expectantly, "Well?"

"It's a long story," Arya dropped down beside her, planting her face in a quilt that smelled faintly of sandalwood. "I got to her just in time, but he tried to attack me as well." She hadn't told her parents that. "Roni was completely freaked out, she wasn't moving or doing anything. I...I know how to defend myself, but this was the first time I had been in a real situation and..."

Page image

187

Her grandmother's soft hand gently traced the faint bruise around the side of her jaw. Arya had taken her hair out its ponytail previously, disguising the purplish stain from her parents. She hated anyone seeing her truly vulnerable, but she could never hide anything from Achamma. "I got Roni out of there, informed the bouncers, but they said nobody by that description had exited the club, as yet, so then they called the police to lock the place down. I only wish that man hadn't escaped."

"He will be caught eventually," her grandmother murmured, "Here, at least, this sort of thing is dealt with fairly. In India, the matter would likely have been hushed up. I'm glad you told the police...how is Roni?"

"Not good," Arya shook her head, "She wouldn't talk at all...I spoke to her mother, told her what happened."

"We all deal with these situations differently."

A buzzing sound from her pocket startled Arya. She pulled out her phone, checking the screen. "Roni," she read aloud, relieved. Getting up from the bed, she moved to the other end of the room for some privacy.

"Hello?"

"Arya...hey," her friend spoke softly, "Are you doing okay?"

"I should be the one asking you that. I wanted to kill that son of a bitch, I swear, if –"

"That's what I wanted to talk to you about, Arya, I mean, do you remember nothing?"

"What do you mean?"

"I mean, when you were talking to the bouncers, the cops...you didn't mention *it* at all...and I was too freaked out to say anything, but I thought maybe you didn't want to tell them, they wouldn't believe you..."

"Roni." She was confused by her friend's disjointed ramble, "I have no idea what you're referring to."

"Arya...that thing that attacked me...it wasn't human," her friend took an audibly shuddering breath, "I know what I saw. He had horns...and fangs..."

"Roni, are you sure he didn't drug you?"

"The cops already tested me for drugs, Arya, I'm not high. Listen to me, when he grabbed me from the club and took me down, how do you think we got there so fast? It wasn't human, it was – something else. And when you screamed, your eyes were red. Like bright red, that wasn't normal either. And he didn't run away or anything like that."

It was the trauma, Arya decided. "What do you mean? He was gone."

"That's just it, Arya. He – it – is gone. When you screamed, you consumed him."

Arya hung up, turning to her grandmother, who was feigning great interest in a book on the four *Vedas*. "I think I'll need to see Roni tomorrow, she seems really freaked out."

"Hmm?"

Arya rolled her eyes, "I know you were listening in on the whole thing."

"I don't know what you're speaking of," her grandmother removed her spectacles with great dignity, "But go on. Is the poor girl alright?"

"She's delusional. She doesn't know what she saw...she thinks the guy that attacked her was some sort of monster...with horns and fangs."

"Oh dear," Achamma appeared disturbed, straightening her posture.

"That's not all," Arya paced around the room, "She said I just sort of engulfed him whole when I screamed."

Her grandmother looked uncharacteristically shaken. Arya quickly

189

approached her, "Are you okay? I know, it's scary, Roni seems completely traumatized, she's going to have to see someone –"

"Arya," the older woman took a deep breath, "Listen to me. I know this all sounds strange, but –"

"Don't tell me you believe her?"

"Have you learned nothing from all the stories I read to you when you were a child? The origin stories, how we came to be?"

Her family members were all practicing Hindus, but she had forgone the weekly visits to the temple a few years ago. She didn't believe in all-powerful gods and goddesses, the demons that combatted them in ancient wars, the tales of boons and sacrifice. "Those aren't real, Achamma, they're more like...extended metaphors."

"Don't give me the nonsense they've fed you in school, child! Now for a minute, please just hear me out. What do you remember, from the stories I told you? About the gods and goddesses?"

Arya decided to humour her for the time being, reciting from memory, "There's the *Trimurti*, the trinity of Shiva, Brahma and Vishnu. And the *Trivedi*, of Saraswati, Lakshmi and Parvati."

Her grandmother reached for two of the small figures from the book-case. She held up the statue of a bare-chested woman, her hips jutting to the side, with her thumb and middle finger joined at their tips. "And what do you know of Parvati?"

"She's supposed to be Shiva's wife and equal...how is this important right now?"

"Who is this?" The other figure she held was markedly different. A ten-armed woman clasped a long sword, a sickle, and an assortment of other objects, including a human head. Her tongue stretched out in a grimace and her hair spread outwards in an untamed mass. She was clad in a necklace of skulls and a skirt of skeletal arms. A man lay sprawled under her foot – Shiva.

"Kali. One of Parvati's forms. She's seen as a protector, a warrior and a destroyer of evil forces. Also associated with sexuality."

"So you haven't forgotten everything I've taught you."

"That doesn't mean I believe any of it!" Arya retorted.

"Don't be foolish, child. Use that brain of yours and think. What is life after death? Our bodies may wither and rot away, but our souls remain preserved, until we are born again."

"Reincarnation."

"Precisely. Until we have completely freed ourselves from vice and sin, our souls continue to pass on to new bodies."

"And you think I'm a reincarnation of…"

"The goddess Kali, yes."

Arya stared at her grandmother for a moment, suspended in incredulity, as she sought the words to politely, but firmly, reject the notion. "Achamma, listen, I don't mean to make light of religion, but your beliefs are your own," Arya pleaded, "I don't share them." She didn't want to offend the older woman, but the idea was ludicrous.

Her grandmother cast her gaze upwards, muttering something under her breath that sounded suspiciously like a prayer for forbearance, before turning back to face Arya. "Did you know Hinduism is considered the oldest religion in the world, by many scholars and historians? Our roots stretch back for centuries and yet you still doubt? Your friend, Roni, she said you consumed the creature, didn't she? If you recall, there is a tale of Kali defeating the demon, Raktabija, and his army?"

"He was undefeatable because every drop of blood of his that was spilt…would produce a clone of himself."

"And how did Kali defeat him?"

"She drank his blood." Arya could see a flimsy vein between this line of thought and Roni's hallucination. "So you're saying I'm some sort of cannibal?"

"Not a cannibal, oh no. You ate a demon, dear. That's an entirely different matter."

~

A rya lay in her bed, unable to sleep. She felt disturbed, and not solely from the events that had transpired at the club that night, but from Roni and her grandmother's words as well. The only monsters she believed existed were murderers, rapists and other fiends. Human predators.

If she was truly a reincarnation of a warrior goddess, wouldn't her so-called "powers" have manifested long ago? Then again, she recalled hearing her literature professor explain the hero's cycle. There was always some sort of triggering point. Anger, loss, pain. She thumped her head into her pillow with a groan, she couldn't possibly be considering this.

She turned over to her other side, facing her window, determined to get some sleep, but a shadow crossed her vision.

The muscled, tattooed bouncer from earlier surveyed her calmly, "Hello, Kali."

She opened her mouth to scream, but he had somehow managed to press a blade to her jugular.

"How the fuck did you get in here?" she breathed, even as her hand automatically reached behind her for the Swiss army knife on her side table.

"How am I here at all?" his tone was oddly petulant, "You thought you drank every last drop of my blood, didn't you?"

"You're insane." Her heartbeat stuttered at the familiar words.

The man cocked his head at her curiously, before a slow smile stretched his lips, "How interesting. You're a clean slate. The others had their memories intact."

"What are you talking about?" she hissed.

"You're a manifestation of the goddess Kali, the warrior and protector," he stated simply, "Though of course, you won't believe me. Humans in this century always want science and reason, even when the truth glares at them in the—"

Arya swung her knife and slashed him across the throat. He looked startled, blood gushing from the open wound in a dark fountain, then laughed, "Foolish girl."

For the first time that night, Arya began to doubt her own sanity.

Naked, horned creatures began to swarm around him, each bearing striking serpentine tattoos that danced under their skin like veins, like the rapist at the club. Dust collected into bare feet, muscled, hairless frames. Golden horns sprouted from their smooth pale heads, twisting into fluted spirals. They gleamed with strange beauty in the pool of moonlight flooding her room.

She opened her mouth in a silent scream. The creatures drew alarmingly closer, then vanished in a sudden instant. All at once, none remained but the bouncer, who stared at her calmly. His throat wound had already faded to a puckered scar. He touched cold fingers to her mouth and then held them up for her to see. They were coated in blood. How strange, she thought weakly, when her mouth tasted of nothing but ash.

"Weak." The bouncer stepped away from the bed, chuckling. "You are not the adversary I was expecting. When *Kali* emerges in all her glory…" he enunciated the name with relish, "I will be there." He opened her window, stood on the ledge and leaped.

A dream...a dream...a dream...

Sunlight trickled in through the shade of her curtains and she could hear the muted chirping of birds outside. It was early morning. She considered burrowing deeper under the covers, but she was awake and unlikely to fall back to sleep anytime soon. She flung back the blankets and rose, advancing towards the window warily.

No one was there, but the window was open. No monstrous body splayed on the ground from an impromptu suicide jump.

She turned back to her bed and froze. Blood stained her blankets. She swiftly pulled down her sweats to check her underwear, but her panties were clean.

"Well, fuck."

Tiny dark red drops splattered her oversized pyjama t-shirt as well. She tugged it off frantically, turning to catch sight of herself in a mirror - wide-eyed, gaunt...with a reddish mark disfiguring her collarbone. She approached the mirror slowly to get a closer look; the colouring resembled that of a henna tattoo, but instead of curling vines and flowers, the stain was clearly in the shape of a skull.

Arya's heart thudded as she recalled Achamma's statue of Kali and her garland of severed human heads. The rapist at the club. The bouncer in her room. *When Kali emerges in all her glory,* he said. She shakily traced the tattoo and dragged her index finger around her neck.

Perhaps it was time she visited the temple after all.

WE ARE ALL GHOSTS

LILY CHANG

There is an alternate me living in a different city, breathing some other air. Our lives are parallel. I know this because we began as one. An individual. Like dandelion seeds, we broke, at different points in time, into multiples, flung onto separate paths. The breaking continues, claiming more realms of possibilities than time can accommodate. Out of these possibilities, only one is sacred, oblivious, and hopeful; all others are ghosts.

Livia has a life growing inside her. In the North American city in which she lives, someone loves her. They are married. They have a big house with a lawn and a deck. No mutated roaches with wings. No stink of sewage. The sky isn't bulbous with pollution. She feels the baby kneading, like a cat does to a blanket. I feel the twist of secrets in my stomach. There are rumours to deflect. *Why haven't you secured a husband yet?* In my country, single women over thirty are considered leftovers. No one is hungry enough for them.

Livia and I began as one in Taiwan. We grew up in Taipei, the capital city. Our home was a cramped two-bedroom in an old apartment building. Our bedroom window was a tiny mouth silenced by grilles. The wallpaper was made of mildew. The kitchen, where our mother sneaked cigarettes, sweated soy sauce fumes. Two blocks away was

Chiang Kai-shek Memorial Park, where we played without our parents worrying about incoming mopeds. We leapt off the park's sturdy trees with our swordplay. Traffic was hushed by the foliage. The air, quiet, became malleable under our feet. On the park's expansive grounds, our robe billowed from our battle aura. If cousin Charlie was with us, he was Zhan Zhao, the greatest knight-errant. The park rendered his shoehorn a sword, his fear of the dark a supernatural quirk. The park disciplined Livia and me to practice our magic as Madam White Snake. It later participated in our rupture, but we didn't know it at the time.

Livia remains oblivious. If she thinks of alternate lives at all, she'll think the moment of rupture was much later, out of our control. A circumstance, like our father deciding to emigrate. It was, in fact, internal, marked by a small movement. A look. I looked. Livia did not.

The breaking of a self begins subtly, like sleep. Senses are reduced and doubled. A sensation, in hesitating, falls behind its facsimile. With time, the split grows ugly, into an uneven tear that hasn't made up its mind about becoming two. The edges of one become lighter, like paper, until its whole existence has thinned into a scream that the world of the other refuses to hear. Something is irrevocably lost.

It's analogous to that first recognition of difference. Before our rupture, we learned how to be the same as our peers in elementary school. A low test score was an anomaly corrected by a hard pinch and twist of an earlobe. A toot from a whistle whisked all our lacklustre feet to attention in any hallway. On Monday mornings they needed to be a hip's distance apart out on the grounds under the sun. We stood in perfect lines, collecting heat strokes to the beat of the national anthem as if they were stamps on bubble tea loyalty cards. Despite the daily uniforms and the chin-length haircuts, Livia and I felt the advent of difference. Subtle, then ugly as a nightmare. It urged us to climb over the surrounding fence of our school one day during recess. We left sameness behind, first a half step, then a full step.

We ran towards the park together. One chest rose and fell. The wind was cool against our sweat, cowering from our battle aura. It watched in awe as we dived into a pond, renouncing our human flesh for pearl-white reptilian scales.

We never made it to the park. The teacher found us at the traffic lights. She muttered incantations and bound us in power-stripping ribbons. The sameness we left behind had told on us. The teacher dragged us into class, smoking a confession out of us with her ancient proverb: *brave enough to do it, not brave enough to own it*. The reward for bravery was the splitting of our palms against her rod as the whole class watched. An ugly, uneven tear. Livia and I did not pretend-cry. No Zhan Zhao to save us. Our desire to disappear before unblinking, hungering eyes was one and the same.

To disappear was to be the same as our peers. When our classmates pressured us to show them our sparring sites in the park that day, we said *yes*. *No* would've been conspicuous.

In her North American three-storey house, Livia paints the park from memory. The oils, with their richness, render the marble walls that line the park white and smooth. The walls' blue shingles, manipulated by perspective, appear infinite. She makes the leaves beckon in Prussian green, as if unburdened by exhaust. The ponds house more orange koi fish than water. She thinks she can distinguish a hint of white scales amidst the orange. Next to it, she adds a squiggle of teal. Sitting back, she wonders which technique to use to depict the sounds she hears. The fish thrashing against one another, fighting for feed. The wind belting the cobblestones in the same way as a swordsman on horseback. The calmness of the woods. The bark of the trees she used to climb is rough but cool against her palms. When she's finished painting, parts of the park are ridged into her nails. She does not wash them off.

I see the park on my way to work every weekday. From the bus window, it looks the same as it is painted in another timeline. I've not entered its grounds since the day of our rupture. There are gaggles of tourists bottlenecked at its turnstile entrances. The park has been renamed but its walls and shingles remain unchanged. Frozen despite the heat. The secret to perpetual youth is not hidden in celestial peaches or the dew from a chrysanthemum. It does not bookend an arduous pilgrimage across jiang hu. It's in our taxes. At noon, the restoration workers eat their buns in the shade. They side-eye young girls in uniforms as they pass. At my grandmother's house, my shoehorns are hung against the wall on a nail.

Tonight will be the first time I've entered the park since that day. Sitting on the bus that I take every weekday from Jinshan, I find that my grandmother has sneaked wads of bills, a pollution mask, and an assault whistle into my purse. Normally she sneaks only cash and a pollution mask. She's lived in the same house in the countryside for the last sixty years. No one locks their doors at night. The neighbours prefer to hurt each other with words.

When my parents and I first moved into my grandmother's house during the recession, I turned the lock every night before bed. For a week, I wore a pollution mask to the market, not noticing I was the only one. Proximity to the sea seems to purify the air a little, but not the noise. In my grandmother's house, the words of my aunts, uncles, and cousins thrash like fish. When there are more people than space, a greeting sounds defensive. When people buy things at the market, they slip noise out of their wallets. A bushel of ripe waxed apples costs the story of our neighbour caught cheating with our other neighbour, yelled across the displays. As in the cities, wealth is the revving of engines, the coughing of exhaust, the barking of abandoned dogs. Generous are the voices urging me to snare a man and make a family. They rattle the edges of my body, pushing me backwards. Soon I will teeter. Carried off into the void of sameness. Disappear.

The route to Taipei begins by coiling around mountains, walloped by the sea on one side. In the compact mirror, my reflection refuses to be still. I am multiple in the glass. The woman across the aisle winks at her phone, purses her lips, presses her thumb and index finger together to make a small heart sign. I watch her repeat the ritual twenty more times. The woman in the row ahead of her does the same. In our representations, we all have double eyelids, enlarged pupils, and whitened skin no longer blemished by sun spots and acne scars. The same filters. The same cosmetic surgeon. Last week, my co-worker brought me to her specialist. He had trained with the best in the art of lasers. He was known for his blade-wielding skills too. In less than half an hour, he could cut the corners of my eyes and make me look beautiful. If Livia could see me, she would not know we had once been singular.

She eats her lunch on the deck. She doesn't have to take small bites. She chews openly. In her country, femininity doesn't escape through her mouth if she fails to cover it when laughing. When she first met her in-laws before they were in-laws, she wore a long, loose white dress and comfortable shoes. Her arms, sleeved in Chinese folktale tattoos, had scales. They told her she was beautiful. Enchanting. They wanted to hear the myths. How a white snake spirit transformed into a woman to save the life of a green snake, who later became her side-kick, Little Teal. How the two journeyed to Mount Emei to steal a magical herb that could restore the life of Madam White Snake's husband, Xu Xian. At dinner, the mother asked how she kept her hair so shiny, thick, and black. Her own hair was wispy, dull, and blonde. Before dinner was over, the mother wanted to give her clothes that didn't fit her anymore. *I haven't been able to wear petite sizes in two decades.* She accepted them, but they weren't quite her style.

At a certain point, Livia chews mechanically, no longer hungry. She keeps eating. She eats until the baby is full. The smoothie that her grandmother-in-law made sticks to her throat like wet grass. Vitamin D seeps into her flesh from the sun. Through her sunglasses, her legs look orange.

When Livia left Taiwan, flying for the first time, she saw the island through the airplane window: minuscule, mildewed, with billows of grey hiding any sign of life. It was malleable between her fingers. She could flatten it, pocket it, and un-shrink it later. In the first few days of arrival, she felt my constant grasps at her edges. A lag. A doubling back on the island. She might have heard my screams in her sleep. She would wake up, feeling heavy. I was becoming light as paper. She would slide down the staircase banister. Her weight rushed her to the bottom. In her parents' new North American house, the space between the carpet and the ceiling on the first floor was wide enough for two storeys. Every day, she practiced her swordplay upside-down, leaping over chandeliers. Her powers surpassed cousin Charlie's in a week. Her mother, who now sneaked cigarettes in the basement, the backyard, and against the garage; cooked and cleaned below her, undisturbed. After a month, it snowed. The foreign substance was beautiful, enchanting. It scaled windows. Enlivened her with freezing spells. It was soft like shaved ice. Hard like marble. She spent hours in the whiteness. The island remained flattened in her pocket.

Snow can fall on Jade Mountain in the winter. On a field trip during middle school, I touched some on a rock. It was March. The snow was unexpected. My classmates and I formed a line to take pictures with a generously peppered boulder. In my hands, the snow became luke-warm. The air, however, tasted pure, untouched. We climbed until the smog was at our feet. The air jolted my lungs. My senses, grounded. For a few moments, looking down at the island, I could be hopeful. Eventually, we headed back down.

I wake up as the bus gets off the freeway. The mountains are timelines away. Taipei is close. Like clockwork, my eyes search for the building with the broken neon sign on the roof. I am looking for a man, seconds before he dives and bursts against the concrete. Before his sinews become kaleidoscopic in the flash of cameras. I never find him. When we ran from our classmates that day in the park, we saw ourselves perched at the edge of the roof. Every step away from our classmates was one step closer to falling. I looked back. Livia did not. My heartbeat half-stumbled, shuffling a step behind a strange, sepa-rate heartbeat.

Our classmates did not want to spar. The girls leaned against the trees, swaying in their silken robes. They all wanted to be the Weaver Girl, but some had to settle for Lady Meng Jiang, Zhu Yingtai, and Little Teal. The boys jabbed at worms in the soil until Weaver Girl assigned them each a character. Qi Liang, his bones mortared in the Great Wall, was to be mourned by Lady Meng Jiang. Liang Shanbo had to open his grave and catch Zhu Yingtai in his arms before both re-emerged as butterflies. The Cowherd and the Weaver Girl were to share a kiss on a bridge of magpies over the Milky Way. And because there were more girls than boys, Madam White Snake and Little Teal could take turns falling in love with Xu Xian under his umbrella. The park was silent as sameness fenced us within its woods. *Why aren't you kissing him, Livia? She wants to kiss Little Teal. Have sex with her. Make babies with her.*

The man on the roof was an actor. He had rumours to deflect. Paparazzi dragged him onto the roof before unblinking, hungering eyes. Smoked a confession out with a proverb: *brave enough to do it, not brave enough to own it.* The reward for bravery was the splitting of his head against the concrete, as the whole country watched. In Taiwan, no one is more generous than news stations, who repeat their stories every hour. For a while, we thought we saw a man on the roof of every building we came across. What did the ground look like from where he was standing? Could he see people, minuscule, teeming, clambering over one another? Feel the smog push against his back? Was he weightless? Or was his life, out of all possibilities, the only sacred one? Eventually, he headed back down.

Our grandmother turned off the TV whenever the news came on. When we visited her in Jinshan, she made us read folktales to her. She never learned to read. Every tale was proof that all men were cheating, lying bastards resembling our grandfather. He forced her into marriage. She refused to let him touch her for thirty years. A powerful, unteachable spell. He died alone in his separate bedroom. We listened, our eyes wide. Her laughter, rough and cool, grew to the corners of the room, penetrating walls, flattening all other noise. It extended to Livia that day when we ran from our classmates. I could not hear it.

Livia, warm and tired, sits inside. Her eyes remain fixed on the back-yard through the window. The baby is trying to kick its way out. Her wife, home from work, makes her another shake in the kitchen. The roar of the blender is folded within the walls. It sounds timelines away. Maybe Livia is on the bus to Taipei, nearing the park. Maybe Livia gets off at the right stop, fixes her skirt, and walks toward the white walls and blue shingles. I am in the three-storey house with the empty bedrooms. The beautiful staircase does not creak. The lush carpeting dulls any sign of life. As is often in the last few months, I stare at the brightness: the sunlit grass, the unmoving skies, the fence in the distance. They stare back at me.

At the airport, before flying for the first time, I looked at the faces of those we were leaving behind. I saw my nose in cousin Charlie's red, sniffly one. My mouth, multiplied on my aunts, said silent goodbyes. My eyes, reflecting my grandmother's, tried to memorize the path of her wrinkles. Sometimes I see her in the backyard. Her spine is curved. Her knees are swollen. She can hardly walk. Sometimes I see cousin Charlie in the shrubs. He dawdles. Instead of hurtling into a truck on his moped, he flicks the grass with a shoehorn. Sometimes I see all of them. Echoes of myself. Instead of the alienating brightness.

At the wedding reception, my in-laws decorated the hall with chopsticks. They meant well, my wife assured me. I asked if forks had a special place in their hearts. She stuffed cake into my mouth. The guests wanted to know where I was from, originally; if I wore the pants in the relationship; if all other Orientals were lactose-intolerant like me. *Why don't you have an accent?* They wanted to hear the myths. How my father transformed me into an English-speaking parrot to impress his immigrant friends. How I learned to be a banana at school. How I lost the ability to change myself back. Before the reception was over, the guests begged me to transform their names into logograms. *This is the Chinese name for Jacqueline. The first character means "horse," the second "strength," the third "tranquillity."* The guests wore my lies as if they were blessings. When the magic came to a close, they trashed the blessings on their way out, returning to sameness.

A month before I graduated from university, my father threw out all my English books. I had contracted difference from reading. It made me forget my Chinese, talk back to the patriarch, and desecrate my flesh with ink as if I owned my body. It made me feverish for women. He tossed them all, wishing for an alternate path, an alternate me. I moved out of his North American three-storey house. Walked myself down the aisle.

Livia waits at the turnstiles. Cousin Charlie is calling. Their grandmother has a bad feeling. There is still time. Charlie can whisk her away on his moped. I hold my breath. I'm hoping to hear his voice. Clear and strong. Not muffled by blood or collapsed flesh. The cremation is on Thursday. Wednesday in North America. My parents will be there. They will burn incense. Fold paper lotus flowers with my aunts and uncles. Fill my grandmother's house with noise. I will be in the three-storey house with the empty bedrooms. Grounded by the life inside of me. Doubled, reduced. My body is not my own.

Livia does not pick up. No Zhan Zhao to save us. She is meeting a man. The son of her father's colleague. He doesn't mind leftovers, if she looks like her picture. Not everyone looks like their pictures. He's hoping she can deliver the happiness promised by her body. If I were hopeful, I might hope for the same. Lean against the wall painted forever white. Sway my skirt. Wait for this timeline to end.

Out of all possibilities, maybe none are sacred, oblivious, or hopeful. Maybe we are all ghosts.

ABOUT THE AUTHORS

Lily Chang - *We Are All Ghosts*

Lily Chang is a writer, editor, and filmmaker based in Montréal, Québec. She is a graduate of Concordia University's MA program in creative writing. Her work has appeared in *Headlight Anthology*, Frog Hollow Press's *The City Series, Dark Helix Ezine*, and elsewhere. She is a finalist for the 2018 CBC Nonfiction Prize and the Speculative Literature Foundation's 2018 Diverse Writers Grant.

~

Urania Fung - *A Debate over the Hopping Undead*

Urania Fung is an English professor who grew up in Texas with 1980s Hong Kong entertainment as her babysitters. Monsters and martial arts have been swimming in her head ever since. For more on what she does besides grading papers, please see her blog at uraniafung.blogspot.com.

~

C arlo Javier - *Janitors*

Carlo Javier is a writer, web developer, and communications specialist based in Vancouver, Canada. He likes to write about issues surrounding the Filipino diaspora, social media, and relationships. *Janitors* marks his first published fiction piece.

~

A nais Jay - *This Other Water*

Anais Jay is a Filipino entrepreneur who reads and writes fiction to keep her sanity. When she was a little girl, she wanted to be a doctor, a lawyer, and a soldier. Fortunately, she can be all of those and more by being a writer. Her short stories have been published in *Toasted Cheese Literary Journal*, *The Vignette Review*, and in Curtiss Bausse's anthology, *Second Taste*. She currently has a post-apocalyptic short story forthcoming in *Philippine Speculative Fiction Volume 12*. Get more doses of strange fiction from her Facebook Page (@AnaisJay-Writes) and her IG (@AnaisJay_Writes).

~

G abriela Lee - *So You Want a Revolution?*

Born and bred in Manila, Philippines, Gabriela Lee's first collection of short stories, *Instructions on How to Disappear: Stories*, was published in 2016 by Visprint, Inc. Prior to this, her work has been published in anthologies and publications in the Philippines, the United States, Australia, and Canada, including in *LONTAR: The Southeast Asian Journal of Speculative Fiction* and *Where the Stars Rise: Asian Science Fiction and Fantasy Stories*. She currently teaches English literature, composition, and creative writing at the University of the Philippines. You can find out more about her at. www.sundialgirl.com

~

S erah Louis - *Unveiling the Night*

Serah Louis is a 21-year-old Canadian writer of Indian descent. She is currently studying Biology and Professional Writing and Communications at the University of Toronto, Mississauga campus. She loves homemade biriyani and a good cup of chai and you'll find her bookshelf cluttered with works ranging from J.R.R. Tolkien to Rabindranath Tagore.

~

L illian Lu – *Heirlooms*

Lillian Lu is pursuing a Ph.D. in English at the University of California, Los Angeles. Her research focuses on eighteenth- and nineteenth-century British literature, gender, and imperialism. She has also written for *The Rambling*.

~

D erwin Mak - *The House of Hagfish*

Derwin Mak's story "Transubstantiation" won the Aurora Award for Best Short Fiction. The anthology *The Dragon and the Stars*, edited by Derwin and Eric Choi, won the Aurora Award for Best Related Work. *Where the Stars Rise*, edited by Lucas Law and Derwin, won the Alberta Book Publishers Award for Speculative Fiction. The anthologies have stories by overseas Chinese or Asian writers to get their viewpoints and experiences in science fiction and fantasy. His novels *The Moon Under Her Feet* and *The Shrine of the Siren Stone* are available again from Dark Helix Press. Derwin's stories have a range of topics, especially the interaction of religion with science and politics. www.derwinmaksf.com

~

J.A.W. McCarthy – *Luksaw*

J.A.W. McCarthy goes by Jen when she is not writing. She lives with her husband and assistant cat in the Pacific Northwest, a place that inspires her dark tales. Her work has appeared or is forthcoming in numerous publications, including *She's Lost Control, Nightscript, Vastarien,* and Flame Tree Publishing's *Lost Souls*. Find her at www.jawmccarthy.com, or on Instagram @jawmccarthy.

~

Joseph F. Nacino - *On The Road to Biringan*

Joseph F. Nacino writes for a living, but he also creates stories that have been published in international (*Fantasy Magazine, City in the Ice, Kitaab's Asian Speculative Fiction*) and local publications (*the Philippine Speculative Fiction series, A Time of Dragons, Friendzones,* etc.). He's also had three anthologies featuring fantasy, science fiction, and horror in the Philippines published online, as ebooks, and in print.

~

I.J.P. Ruiz - *Waking Fire*

I.J.P. Ruiz is a Filipino writer raised in Hong Kong and Singapore. Having graduated from the University of British Columbia, he currently works and lives in Vancouver, Canada. Jacob seeks to explore the concept of Liminality through his work; drawing inspiration from his intercultural background, science fiction, high fantasy, history, and world mythology. In his spare time, Jacob loves exploring the local dining scene, trying new recipes in the kitchen, and diving into a good single player RPG. He also dabbles in logo design.

~

Sylvia Santiago and Jenny Wong - *The Winter Sister*

Sylvia Santiago and Jenny Wong pooled the dark depths of their imaginations to conjure up *The Winter Sister*. Sylvia envisioned Misa as the tortured artist, while Jenny was determined to name Vic after his ultimate fate as . . . the victim. Sylvia's work will be featured in upcoming issues of *Uncanny Magazine* and *Liminality*. Jenny's work has found happy homes in places such as *Luna Station Quarterly, From the Depths,* and *Multiverse - an international anthology of science fiction poetry.* This is their first (but not their last) literary collaboration.

~

Bianca Sayan - *Capable Man*

Bianca's blender-ancestry made her spend too much time figuring out whether she qualified for this anthology. She resides in Toronto, where she tries to, by day, persuade people to share their data, and, by night, write half-way decent speculative fiction. She and her main character in *Capable Man* tend to worry about the same things.

~

Kwan-Ann Tan - *Scenes From the Night Market Across the Sea*

Kwan-Ann Tan is a writer from Malaysia and a student of English at Oxford University. She edits for *Rambutan Literary,* and her work has been published or is forthcoming in places such as *The Poetry Annals, Porridge Magazine, Crab Fat Magazine* and *The First Line.* You can find her on Twitter at @KwanAnnTan and more of her work at https://kwananntan.carrd.co/.

~

Vincent Ternida - *Not All Bears Drink Mead*

Emerging author Vincent Ternida's pieces have appeared in *Ricepaper* Magazine, Dark Helix Press, and was longlisted for the CBC Short Story Prize in 2019. Ternida's first novella, *The Seven Muses of Harry Salcedo*, was published by Asian Canadian Writer's Workshop and Dark Helix Press. He currently has a collection of short stories in development. He lives in Vancouver, British Columbia.

ABOUT THE TEAM

J F GARRARD - EDITOR

JF is the founder of Dark Helix Press, Co-President of the Toronto branch of the Canadian Authors Association, Deputy Editor for *Ricepaper Magazine* and Assistant Editor for *Amazing Stories Magazine*. She is an editor and writer of speculative fiction (*Futuristic Canada, Trump: Utopia or Dystopia, The Undead Sorceress, Ricepaper Issue 19.3*), non-fiction (*The Literary Elephant*). Her latest published short stories includes *The Curse* in the *Brave New Girls: Adventures of Gals and Gizmos* anthology, *The Metamorphosis of Nova* in the *Blood Is Thicker* anthology by Iguana Books and *The Perfect Husband* in the *We Shall Be Monsters* Frankenstein anthology by Renaissance Press. *jfgarrard.com*

~

A LLAN CHO - EDITOR

Allan Cho is an academic librarian at the University of British Columbia and an instructor at the University of the Fraser Valley. Allan is actively engaged in a number of initiatives in the community and has served on the board of the Asian Canadian Writers' Workshop Society (ACWW), Chinese Canadian Historical Society of British Columbia (CCHSBC) and Vancouver Asian Heritage Month Society (VAHMS). He has written for the *Georgia Straight, Diverse Magazine,* and *Ricepaper.* His fiction has appeared in the anthologies, *The Strangers* and *Eating Stories: A Chinese Canadian and Aboriginal Potluck.*

~

William Tham - Editor

William Tham Wai Liang was the Senior Editor of *Ricepaper.* He is also the author of *Kings of Petaling Street* and his second novel is due for release in early 2020. He is currently based in George Town, Penang.

~

Lea Duck - cover designer & illustrator

Lea Duck has creative mind with a nerdy soul. She is a graphic designer and illustrator based in Vancouver, British Columbia. Her obsession with design (and fantasy) started long ago when she was four years old at the Northern Alberta Institute of Technology. She wasn't a child prodigy already attending college, but rather, her mother was a professor of graphic design. She always looked forward to the days her mother would take her into work because she would get full run of the art room. She is now following in my mother's duckprints. She holds a Bachelor's Degree in Art from Vancouver Island University and has six years of experience in the graphic design industry. You can follow her on instagram @lea.duck.creative or check out her portfolio online at www.leaduck.com.

ABOUT RICEPAPER

R icepaper first began as a newsletter for the Asian Canadian Writers' Workshop (ACWW)—eight pages which were photocopied back-to-back and stapled together. It was a way for ACWW members to communicate with each other as well as celebrate individual successes. ACWW, a non-profit organization, continues to operate and publish *Ricepaper* today. From these humble beginnings, *Ricepaper* became a quarterly magazine that was distributed coast-to-coast, featuring new voices emerging from the Asian Canadian arts and literary community. With advancements in technology, *Ricepaper* then moved online, thus affording writers a wider audience and richer medium to deliver ideas.

Recently, it has begun to focus on publishing anthologies, novels, and other full-length works while maintaining its existing web presence. Therefore, *Ricepaper* continues to be the longest running literary organization of its kind with an Asian Canadian perspective.

Visit us at ricepapermagazine.ca to read the latest stories and Asian culture content. We are constantly looking for new voices!

www.ingramcontent.com/pod-product-compliance
Lightning Source LLC
Chambersburg PA
CBHW060638260626
47161CB00008B/2910